CLOUD FORTRESS

A RUCKSACK UNIVERSE NOVEL

ANTHONY ST. CLAIR

RUCKSACK PRESS

"If this world is one dream among countless other dreams, then heaven is a dream within that dream. Yet for all the dreams that pass for universe and existence, perhaps none is so fair as the tales of the Heart of the World. A place of kindness and hope—but hidden away from the rest of the wicked world for the sake of its own protection. Perhaps it is a myth. Or perhaps it is waiting for its time to be real again."

   – Guru Deep, *Legends Through the Third Eye*

PART I

POCKET

The train clack-choofed around a hill. Jade looked out the window at her left and watched a mountain move overhead.

White, brown, and gray, the V-shaped cloud looked like a giant mountain—only upside down. Dull, curved puffs covered the broad top, in stark contrast to the otherwise clear blue sky. The sides slanted toward each other as they went down, ending not at a peak but at a broad, jagged expanse of wispy cloud, as if the bottom point had been torn off. Yet the snowy upside-down summit base gleamed as bright white as any Himalayan summit. The speeding cloud seemed to be making its way, like Jade's chugging packed overnight train, northward toward the city of Agamuskara, India. How long would it take the cloud to keep going north? How long before the cloud left India for Nepal—beyond, into the home of the world's tallest peaks, the Himalayas? From there, the world would change, from green and fertile to brown and barren.

The train slowed as it pulled into a station and stopped. Jade and the five fellow travelers she shared the compartment with lurched forward and backward, in time with the train's squealing brakes. Their doorless compartment was near the front of the train car, and some of the travelers she shared with rose and stepped into the corridor. Behind her, to her right, Jade heard the train car's door open. Moments later, people filled the corridor. Station stops were great opportunities to get drinks and food, but Jade wasn't thirsty or hungry. She ignored the young men carrying their steel urns through the train. The scent of the sweetened, spiced hot chai tea wove through Jade's nose and soul. It was almost tempting. So were the fruit, samosas, and other colorful, aromatic, delectable snacks the women on the platform were holding up. But Jade let them pass her by.

The train car held ten compartments like the one where Jade sat. Dull, wide corrugated-metal strips trimmed the edges of the walls and ceilings. The main surfaces of those walls and ceilings were the color of fresh cream, and they gleamed in the sun. Jade sat on a bench seat that could be slept on as a small bed. An identical one was across from her, but was currently empty, as were two other berths above each lowest one. Jade rested her head against the wall, and her gaze wandered beyond the window. The massive cloud blew across the world until it was gone from her sight. Jade imagined the cloud passing through bare skies into the peaks of Tibet, the Roof of the World. There the Indian subcontinent continued its eternal bulldozing into Asia. There the cloud might find its mountain twin.

But Jade knew that wouldn't be the case. Clouds changed. They formed and they dissipated. This massive cloud would expend itself as rain over villages, fields, and cities. That cloud would never see the Himalayas, much less Tibet. In this world, the only thing that stayed the same was the fact that all things change.

Jade's gaze came back to the train. She took in her reflection in the train window. Her long dark hair, brown skin, and gold-ringed blue eyes gleamed in the sun. But Jade herself didn't feel the same either. She had also changed. She felt reborn, newly emerged in the world. Ten years had passed since she left Hong Kong. Well, she left, but not in the usual ways like leaving by a train, bus, or ship. Because the world had stopped. She remembered it all: a blue bird frozen in midair, a leaf halfway from tree to ground.

And him. On one knee. Right arm extended toward her. Inside the open little clamshell box, even the sunlight had paused while glinting on what was inside—

In the train window's reflection, Jade saw something else.

The reflexes from her training took over, and she spun around.

Her hand closed around the wrist of a teenage boy who had sat next to her without making a sound.

"This is the part where you stop." Jade kept her voice soft and her eyes kind, but both words and gaze shone with a hint of something hard and sharp.

The boy's eyes widened as he pulled his hand out of Jade's daypack.

"I'm sorry," said the boy.

Jade shook her head. She looked the boy in the eye. Part of her sight also focused on what was happening around him—and what was right above his head. The floating, twining silver-and-gold helixes told the boy's story. Past and possibility. Truth and lies. She saw what she needed to see. "You don't have to apologize. But you do need to tell me why."

"Agamuskara," he replied.

Jade nodded. She understood. India's holiest and unholiest city. The city that was like the fire of life itself: vibrant and smoky. The boy couldn't be older than eighteen. Jade focused her sight and let her training take over. No. Sixteen.

"You need to make your way in the world," she said.

"But I have no money," he replied. "No family." The train began moving. Jade could hear the train car door open again behind her, followed by low quick exchanges in Hindi, the occasional clink of coins, and a *schnick* sound. By the sound of it, the conductor must have started punching tickets.

"He'll kick me off again," said the boy to Jade. "Last time, they didn't even wait to arrive at the next station. Just dropped me in the middle of nowhere."

The conductor stopped beside them and stared.

Jade handed over her ticket. The boy looked away.

The conductor punched Jade's ticket and handed it back. He held out his hand to the boy. And the conductor smiled, as if savoring the anticipation of what he was about to do.

"Excuse me," said Jade. "How much is a one-way ticket to Agamuskara?"

The conductor's smile vanished. He mumbled the fare. Jade dug into her pocket and handed over the rupees. The conductor grumbled, but he punched the ticket and handed it to the boy. The muttering continued even as the conductor continued down the corridor.

The boy turned toward Jade. "Thank you," he said.

"You're welcome."

"But why?"

Jade smiled and looked at him. She stared not as a person, but as a Jade. She could read the entwined threads of decision and destiny over anyone's head. Running from every person and every being, the threads intertwined with all else. As they flowed like streams, they wove the always-being-woven fabric of existence.

"I see truth in you," said Jade. "How much truth depends on you. Your life hasn't been easy. Agamuskara won't be easy. No matter what the world brings your way, be kind. I ask only one thing. As you make your way, pay this kindness forward as you can, and make a life where you can help others who need it too."

The boy nodded, then stood. "I should go back to third class, before the conductor comes back."

"Why would you do that?"

"My ticket."

Jade smiled. "Look again."

The boy held it up and stared. And stared some more.

Jade patted the seat where he'd been sitting. "This is yours."

He sat back down, bewildered and quiet. Jade picked up her daypack, unzipped it, and reached inside. "I have something for exactly this sort of situation." On the little table jutting out from the window, she set a bottle of soda and a bottle of Galway Pradesh Stout.

"You are many kindnesses," said the boy. "It's a shame India is so hot. Your drinks will be warm, and you deserve something cold and refreshing."

"Oh, that?" Jade grinned. "The world's full of surprises."

She didn't go into detail, of course. It was one thing to thumb her nose at The Management's rules; it was quite another to explain that she was doing so. Jakes and Jades weren't superhuman. The training taught them that. But they did learn certain skills at understanding and manipulating the world. Jade's favorite, other than the ability to listen to any being or object, was touch. Touch any beverage, and she could make it the perfect temperature.

Even beer and soda in a humid Indian train car on a blazing wet hot Indian day.

The bottle was sweating with condensation by the time Jade popped off the cap and handed it to the boy. He shivered as his warm hand closed around the cold glass. "How did you do that?"

Jade chuckled. "It's my favorite superpower."

As he took long fast pulls from the bottle, his eyes widened with each swallow. Jade popped the top off her beer and took a long swallow as well. The stout did as it always did: made the world look a little sharper, a little clearer, a little brighter. Even before becoming a Jade, she heard it said that the world's most popular beer was more than a beer. It was a way of understanding reality.

As a Jade, she now understood how true that was.

"Are you going to Agamuskara too?"

Jade looked back at the boy. "Yes I am," she replied. "Like you, I'm making my way in the world. I'm on my way to a job there."

"Where will you be working?"

"At the Everest Base Camp Pub and Hostel," she replied. "I'm the new bartender."

"Everest Base Camp?" The boy whistled. "Even I've heard of that place."

Jade didn't add that along with serving drinks, she'd be reading people's destinies and decisions. Then she'd give them the right nudge toward the path that the world needed them to take.

"Wow," said the boy. "You must be very good at what you do."

Jade shrugged. "I suppose that's what we'll find out." She tried to keep to herself the disquiet in her heart.

"You don't sound so certain."

Jade sighed. "I wish I did. Truth is, I took this job a while back. At the time I thought for certain it was the right thing to do, but sometimes, even now, I doubt. This is the first time I've done a job like this. There's a lot more responsibility than you might think. I hope I do the right thing."

The boy shrugged. "You have nothing to worry about."

"I hope you're right," Jade replied.

For a while they sat there in silence, looking out the window and enjoying their cold drinks. Jade thought of all the things she hadn't told the boy. The things she wouldn't tell anyone.

Like when the world had paused on that day ten years ago, and three hooded figures had appeared before Jade. She couldn't see their faces. Even now she didn't know if they had faces. She didn't know anything about them. She didn't even know if they were human.

She didn't mention what they had asked her. How they had offered her an amazing job: to be a Jade, an agent of destiny and decision. She would be one of many around the world who influenced destiny and decision. She would be among those who helped keep life itself on track.

There was a catch, of course.

She had to give up her old life for a completely new one. Not that it was an undesirable exchange. Rather a good one, really. When she was a teenager she'd run away from where she grew up —she refused to call it home. She'd wandered for a couple of years, then had made her way to the independent city-nation of Hong Kong. She'd loved the mix of cultures there, like many streams flowing into a grand lake. She'd liked working odd jobs. Keeping her head down. Really, though, none of it was hard to leave behind.

No. That wasn't true. There had been one thing. One person.

Regardless, in this new life, she herself would not age or get ill. She could understand any language. She was stronger than a typical human, and her mind was faster too. She especially loved that part. She'd always appreciated her mind the most. Her mind had kept her going during the long dark shadow of her childhood. Her mind had helped her imagine a world far beyond what her eyes could see. Jade smiled. It still did.

Of course, being a Jade wasn't all pouring whiskey and listening to people's tales of joys and woes. At times it would be a rather high-stress job too. She would often find herself on the world's razor edge of life or death, yes or no, sometimes metaphorically and sometimes all too literally.

But that wasn't the hardest part. Though in some ways it was also the best perk of them all.

Everyone she had ever known believed that she was dead, the victim of a sudden accident. Sure, she felt bad that some people likely felt sad about her being dead. And one person in particular.

While no one would know about her, and some would even forget her, she would never forget one person. The guilt still gnawed at her. She still regretted leaving him there like that. His arm outstretched, his question unanswered. Forever. And she never knew what had become of him.

She didn't say that she had cried when The Management had told her all of this. And that even now, ten years later, the bittersweet guilt remained. Jade doubted it would ever leave.

The hot Indian day began to darken. Jade and the boy watched the sun set, deep red-orange and then gone. Jade bought them dinner from the dining car, and they spoke more of Agamuskara. It was the oldest city in India, and people traveled there from all over to find their way in life.

To repay her kindness, the boy also told Jade a story.

It was an ancient legend about a smiling fire shrouded in darkness. Amidst Agamuskara's bright walls the unknown evil lay at the city's heart. Long ago, a daughter of the Heart of the World had left her family's secret mountain to save the world. In the place that would one day become Agamuskara, she vanquished and imprisoned the evil. She had been pregnant at the time, and her son became a great hero. For thousands of years he wandered the world. He stopped much harm, and in many places changed evil to good. Now he slept in another realm, until the day the darkness again emerged in Agamuskara. Then he would return and face the darkness in a final battle of life or death, of yes or no. On that day, all the world would continue—or fall.

Jade thought it was a wonderful story. Besides, if she kept the boy talking about his life and his dreams, he wouldn't ask questions about her.

The view outside the windows faded, and darkness came over the world. The sounds of conversation, jokes, and games softened, quieted, and faded. Parents got children to bed. Low talk whispered through the train car, along with the occasional clink of bottles.

"Rest easy," said the boy. "I will look after you."

Then he fell asleep against Jade's shoulder.

Jade sat there, smiling and chuckling. She stared at the darkness outside the window and listened to the people on the train drift off to sleep, one by one. Most of them, like her and the boy, were on their way to Agamuskara. Some would continue to other parts of northern India. Come morning, the train would arrive at her destination. Jade would grab her backpack, which contained all her worldly possessions. Then she would catch a taxi to the Everest Base Camp.

Finally, once the train was silent, Jade went to sleep too.

Dawn light woke her, reaching gently across the train car from the window across from where Jade sat. The boy was gone, perhaps off to the toilet—though, to be on the safe side, Jade checked her backpack and daypack. Everything was still where it should be. Jade stretched and looked out the window. Perhaps in the night they had had a delay. Instead of seeing the buildings and streets and traffic of Agamuskara, the view outside the train was rural—all villages, fields, and rivers, including one, she was sure, that was the famous River Agamuskara, for which the city was named.

Jade frowned. The river was flowing south, but at the city it turned east. It didn't make sense that this would be the Agamuskara. Jade looked again to the far window, where the sun rose in the east. If she was seeing the river, then it was flowing south. That could only mean the train was now north of the city.

Leaving her backpack, Jade left her seat. She had to find the conductor and ask when they would be arriving—and where they were.

She stepped into the corridor, and realized something else troubled her.

The train was too quiet.

No sounds of people sleeping. No loud snores or heavy breathing sawed through the air. No children talked in soft sleepy voices with their parents. No one was shuffling back and forth to the toilets.

Her eyes widened.

She peeked back into her compartment.

Not only was the boy gone. Though the berths were all still down in their sleeping positions, no one else was there.

Only Jade.

The train lurched. Jade stumbled and grabbed onto a seat.

Outside the window, the world sped up. The river, the fields, the brightening sky all rushed by now. The train had accelerated to a dangerous speed.

Fear flooded Jade. Her pulse quickened and her breath clacked in and out in rhythm with the wheels.

What was wrong with the train?

She walked through the car but saw no sign of the conductor, nor heard even the slightest sound from another passenger.

And Jade understood.

The entire train was empty.

2

DOOR NO. 2

The world blurred as the train went faster and faster, sending a bolt of panic through Jade. No help or sympathy came from the empty seats and the bare luggage racks.

Heart pounding faster, Jade clutched the back of a seat.

"Is anyone here?"

She knew it was futile, but she had to try.

Silence answered. As she knew it would.

Answers. Answers were what she needed. Who was behind this? Where had everyone gone—and why was she the only one left?

A glance at the wall made her pause. A long, thin, gray chain ran the length of the train car. The emergency stop.

She smiled, and yanked the chain.

Instead of slowing down, the train sped up.

As it did it went over some sort of bump, knocking Jade forward and smacking her head against a seat. Pain welled up in her eyes, but she stood up and fought off the hurt.

Looking behind her and looking ahead, there were two doors, one at the front of the train car and one at the back. Two chances to find some answers. Solid and opaque, the ends of the car were also the only two places where Jade couldn't see what was outside.

She started making her way to the back of the train car. Morning sunlight flashed on the brushed aluminum of the train car's window frames. The metal latch was warm against her hand as Jade stood at the door. She inhaled. She closed and then opened her eyes. And pulled the latch.

The door rolled smoothly open. Beyond it, the train car ended. So did the train. No vestibule between cars. No next car. Nothing but gleaming track. As far as Jade could see, the track trailed back south toward Agamuskara.

The landscape was changing. As the train continued on its northward path, the plains were giving way to hills. The morning light was already a wet blaze, but it was burning off a deeper chill than Jade knew from anywhere else in India.

Everything she knew was behind her now. Where she had been. Where she should be going. All the world she thought she was about to know. Gone. She had no options here. No choices. The speeding train was going far too fast. Leaping off the platform would be fatal. Even if she survived, where would she go? She had no idea where she was, or what might be nearby, and there were no signs of villages. Not so much as a lonely hut.

Even worse, with every clack of the wheels, she was farther and farther from Agamuskara, from any hint of a settlement or civilization. She had no idea where the train was going. Every moment not knowing made her less likely to find her way back.

Closing the door, Jade turned and rested her back against it. The panic exploded now, and she squeezed her eyes shut. Alone. No idea what to do or who had made this happen. Helpless. The fear hadn't been this bad since—

Jade opened her eyes.

"Alone, yes," she said. "But not helpless."

The panic fled. Resolve poured through her. "I am the catalyst of change and choice. I am a Jade of the Jakes and Jades," she said to the empty train. "I chose and was chosen. I carry the secrets of existence. My actions steer the course of decision and destiny." She pulled away from the door and stood straight, stared down the train car, and narrowed her eyes. "And I will find out what's happened to me and who's behind it."

She pushed away the fear. Ten years of training had helped her focus a great deal on being able to push away and to embrace fear and uncertainty. To be alive was to know fear and to know uncertainty. Why fight them? Accept them instead, and you could transform them. Redirect their energies. Learn from them—and make them allies. Jakes and Jades weren't warriors. Nonetheless, their lives revolved around a willingness to deal with hard moments. In crises where existence itself fades or shines, sometimes all life turned on the actions of a Jake or Jade.

Walking through the train car again, Jade started to think through what could be going on.

"Someone could have abducted me," she said. "Some enemy of The Management figured out who I am and thought a rookie Jade would be an easy target."

She shook her head. That didn't make sense. Secrecy and obscurity were at the heart of the Jakes and the Jades. Hardly anyone knew about them or The Management.

It was a test.

The Management were behind it. The final test of a Jake or Jade. The Management had to see how the rookie handled surprise and uncertainty. Plop them in a situation, completely alter it, destroy expectations. See what happens.

Pass. Or fail.

Jade didn't know what was going on or how she would handle it. But she knew one thing: A train didn't drive itself. There had to be an engine car. People would be there. And people would have answers.

She passed by her compartment and stopped for her backpack. Everything was as it should be.

Standing at the front of the train, Jade reached for the door latch but hesitated.

"Whatever is beyond that door," she said, eyes closed and head lowered, "you have to deal with it. One step, one word, one moment at a time. That's your choice. That's your chance."

She opened her eyes. Raised her head. And smiled.

"So take it."

The fear welled up again. "I may not be in Agamuskara at my first post, but that doesn't change who I am," she said. "Stop being afraid. Start being a Jade."

She pulled the latch.

3

KEEP OUT

Beyond the doorway, a short enclosed vestibule led to the train car beyond.

At the other end, a bright red sign on the door said, "Engineer Cab. Keep Out."

The world was full of signs like that. Employees Only. No Trespassing. Keep Out. Many of them, thought Jade with a silent chuckle, were signed "The Management." And no one knew. Hiding in plain sight was the best hiding.

Jade thought of her training. The best part about signs like that? Jakes and Jades knew they weren't warnings. They were invitations.

Opening the door, Jade went inside. The door clicked shut behind her. And locked.

Jade tried the latch, but it didn't move. The fear rose back up, and she fought it back down and turned. A dark-brown, thin, wood-paneled wall blocked Jade from seeing anything beyond.

She stepped to the right of the wall. Inside the train car, a narrow, dim corridor ran the length of the engine car. Beyond the wall, the train's engines screamed and whined at the speed the train was being forced to sustain.

Down, down the corridor she walked. At the end, a patch of light glowed.

Jade left the corridor, and an open compartment lay before her. So did the world. At the front of the engine car, a windscreen spanned the full width of the engine. It wrapped a quarter of the length of each side, and stretched from the ceiling to the top of an instrument panel that rose up from the floor. Covered in switches, dials, buttons, and levers, the panel glowed with little lights. Indicator needles bounced around their dials—or pointed deeper into red areas they should avoid.

Before the instrument panel, the backs of two tall chairs faced her. Before the chairs, though, was the wide blurred world. The train sped through rising hills. The world passed in blurry, alternating shades of brown and green, barren and verdant. The train was also climbing—yet still accelerating.

They approached a sharp curve. To the right of the train, sheer rock rose high. To the left, the world dropped away. Jade saw only a small glimpse of a vast depth. She didn't see the bottom. But she knew that if the train derailed, it would crumple, explode, and kill anyone aboard. Which may yet be only her.

Her breath rose and swelled, rocketing toward her throat. She wanted to yell, to scream, to shriek with raw primal survival. The instinct shoved aside even the training. She tensed to leap toward the instrument panel, to find a way to stop the train. But the rational part of her mind, still in the background, knew there was no stopping the train.

Then they were at the curve.

Metal whined. Jade was certain the right side of the train lifted into the air. The change in force sent her stumbling and staggering.

But they stayed on the track. Soon the curve was nothing but another thing they had passed in a whir, a blur, and a flash. Another thing now passing away behind them.

The train left the foothills. It began moving across a bright yellow plain, the wheat tall and ready to harvest. Ahead, though, beyond the field, she could see them now, for the first time.

The Himalayas. The world's tallest mountains—and among the most remote. The mountains rose in the far but ever closer distance. Closer to the train, she could see some green and brown. Faraway peaks shone with only silvery gray and snowy white.

The chairs swiveled around to face her.

Jade's glance swept back into the engine car. Two men looked at her. They looked identical, most likely twin brothers. And potentially from this region of India, or from around Agamuskara. They puzzled her though.

Their skin seemed a rich terra-cotta brown. Yet a paleness shone from the men, as if they weren't fully there somehow, or as if they didn't have good blood flow. Both of them had short black hair. They wore dark suits. Not black, Jade realized as she looked more closely, but with some brown woven through. Their shirts were a blend of gold and silver, and their ties had alternating blue and green stripes.

"Ah, Jade Agamuskara Bluegold," said one of the men. "It is so nice to meet someone with whom we can speak plainly and openly."

Jade's eyes narrowed. She took a step into the room. All her senses strained to take in everything, every detail, any potential threats. But she sensed no weapons. And no malice in the men's dark eyes. Only a certain—she couldn't help but smile—mischief. But the smile faded. That mischief wove through with a deep sadness, a regret that looked as deep and old as canyons.

"I'm so glad you appreciate plain talk," replied Jade. "I could use some."

When the men smiled, Jade realized they weren't identical. The man sitting to her left had a long, pinkish, jagged scar. Little radiating lines ran like forks of lightning down the right side of his face. The lightning disappeared down his neckline. Jade wondered how long the scar ran. The man sitting to her right had an identical scar, only on the left side of his face.

"This is my brother Mim," said the man on the right, pointing left.

"This is my brother Pim," said the man on the left, pointing right.

"And you already know who I am," said Jade. "Right down to my full name, which isn't exactly on my passport. So who the hell are you? How do you know who I am? Above all, where are you taking me and why?"

Mim smiled. "I knew this would be a good idea," he said to his brother.

Pim nodded. "No disguises for once. No strange voices. Do you know what a relief it can be to wear your own skin for once, and not have to look ridiculous for the sake of messing with someone's mind?"

Jade looked back and forth between them, and had no idea what to say in reply.

"But no matter," said Mim.

"No matter indeed," said Pim. Both the brothers rose.

"You must be parched," said Mim, extending his right arm.

"And famished," said Pim, extending his left arm.

Following their lead, Jade looked over to the rear of the compartment. Three chairs surrounded a small table set with chai, coffee, mugs of Galway Pradesh Stout, and a full, sumptuous breakfast.

Woven through her senses now, Jade's training tuned up high, like the volume on a radio. A perk of the job, The Management had explained. Besides having immunity to diseases, augmented strength, and no aging, Jakes and Jades knew with a glance whether something was safe to eat or drink.

"We know you love chai," said Mim, "but we know you probably won't take it right now."

"So we thought you would like coffee instead," said Pim.

Jade chuckled. "And beer in the morning?"

Mim shrugged. "You haven't yet heard what we have to tell you."

They understood Jakes and Jades very well. Jade did love chai, and many other beverages, but she knew that those would be rare treats during her time as a Jade. Her job, like that of all other Jakes and Jades behind bars around the world, was to influence decision and destiny. They did so with a range of elixirs, kept in secret, unseeable cabinets below their bars. With those elixirs, they could influence any beverage, though the elixirs worked best with alcohol. Alcohol had such a way of bringing out anyone's true interests, dreams, despairs, and desires.

Four drinks, though, were beyond a Jake or Jade's influence.

"Coffee makes you see everything clearly, so it cannot be affected," said Mim, sitting in a chair so his right side faced the compartment wall. "Water is the essence of all life, containing all that is, was, and could be."

"Absinthe is the gateway to dreams beyond," said Pim, sitting opposite his brother. "And stout is reality in a glass, ultimately and always its own immutable self."

"Who sent you?" Jade stood at the edge of the table, across from her chair, between the table and the compartment wall. "How do you know so much about me? About... what I know?"

"You really should sit down," said Mim. "We do have so much to go over."

The sound of Jade's blood rushing through her body drowned out the world, but not her training. She turned away from the brothers and looked out the large front window. Another useful ability was being able—mostly—to tell when people were telling the truth. Mim and Pim spoke curiously... but honestly.

Jade sat down. Poured a cup of coffee, strong and dark. But she took a long swallow of stout first.

"We will tell you what little we can and were instructed to do," said Pim. "Soon we will be at our first destination."

"Our first," said Jade. "Because there are clearly more."

Mim nodded. "There will be three destinations. Hopefully a fourth, and final, one. That depends in part on you. It will pay to remember that sometimes your final destination is where you began."

"Are you about to tell me that you go so that you can return to where you were but understand it for the first time?"

"While we also appreciate T. S. Eliot's poetry," said Pim, "I'm afraid that he isn't always accurate. You might understand it, but you might just know it for the first time instead."

The breakfast was hot and sumptuous, full of succulent aromas. Above all, her Jade senses told her, it was safe.

"Why are you smiling?" asked Mim.

"I'm remembering something one of my teachers told me about traveling," replied Jade. "When you're on the road, you never pass up a chance for a drink, a meal, or the loo."

She pulled over large helpings of food. Mim and Pim ate little.

"As you may have surmised," said Pim, "you don't need to worry about the train. For now the course is set and easy, but we can tend to things if need be."

"I'm afraid that driving the train is the only easy part of this," said Mim.

"We've taken you north into the Himalayas," said Pim. "Out of India and into Tibet."

"Tibet?" Jade set down her coffee and looked out the window. The hills gathered tight around them now, each a little taller than the ones they passed. Far ahead, a village appeared. It seemed so small and fragile against the hills and mountains, like a newborn baby amidst giants.

Jade shook her head. "I'm supposed to be in Agamuskara."

"You will be," said Mim. Sadness flared up in his voice. It even overwhelmed the mischief that had been so plain before. "You will be," he said again. "Assuming you survive and all that."

The train slowed down, then reached a platform and stopped.

4

———

ARRIVAL

The village, or at least what Jade could see of it from the train, was small. Squat buildings, no more than three stories, dotted the area beyond the train station.

"Welcome to the first destination," said Mim. "You are ready to begin."

"Begin what?" Jade shook her head. "I don't even know where we are."

"We are where you need to begin," said Pim. "At least take a look."

"Fine." Having already finished her breakfast, Jade polished off her beer and coffee too. Slinging on her backpack, Jade stared out the front window, then at the strange brothers.

"Are you coming with me?"

"Oh, don't worry about that," said Mim.

"You'll be seeing us for sure," said Pim. "But we need to tidy away the dishes first. Go ahead and take a look around. You're still a traveler, after all. We'll meet you outside."

Going to the end of the corridor, Jade opened a door. The dry thin air of the Himalayas greeted her. Her body adjusted, and she might as well have been at sea level again. Another perk of the job, The Management had explained during the training. A Jake or Jade could adapt to the atmospheric conditions of any habitable part of the planet.

And it hit her. What Pim had said. Still a traveler. Jade had traveled plenty of the world before Hong Kong, before becoming a Jade.

"Here I am," she said, as she stood at the edge of the doorway, the train compartment behind her, a new world before her.

She smiled. The old thrill came back. Somewhere new. Somewhere else. Unknown. To a traveler, the world was a new friend you were starting to get to know.

"Here we go then," said Jade. "Welcome to Don't-Know-Where's-Ville, Tibet. Pleased to meet you."

She stepped off the train.

Standing there, the train behind her, she tried to get her bearings. Beyond the little platform was a small building. A gussied-up shack, and light on the gussy. Presumably some sort of ticket station, it looked shut and no one was around. Past that, and people wandered by a narrow street of brown dirt. No one looked at Jade, or spoke to her, or paid her any attention at all. It was as if they didn't even know she was there.

The thrill of a new place faded almost as quickly as it had come upon her.

"This is nuts," said Jade. "I shouldn't be here. I should be in Agamuskara. I have a job to do. A new job. Unless I'm already sacked, now that I'm not where I'm supposed to be." She turned around. "I have to get back."

Jade stepped back up onto the train and headed toward the engine compartment.

"Mim and Pim," she said as she came toward where they had had their strange breakfast together. "This is wrong. I have to go back. Whatever you think is going on, or whatever your deal is, please, I need to get back to Agamuskara."

But no one was there. Jade looked all around the engine

compartment. There was no other door, or anywhere else they could have gone to without passing her first. She'd never even moved away from the train. She would have heard them pass her by if they had gone down the corridor toward the back end of the train car.

"Where are you?" She knew it was futile, but she had to ask anyway.

No Mim and Pim, though, meant the train wasn't going anywhere.

Jade left the train again. No station employee was at the little building, and Jade couldn't find a train schedule anywhere. When would the train leave again? She had to be on it.

The little panic rose again, but Jade kept it in check. If a train came to a place, a train would leave the place. That was the way with trains. But she still needed something to do, somewhere to be, in the meantime.

Watching the villagers go about their lives, she started walking toward people. She thought back to her training and smiled. Jakes and Jades could comprehend and speak any language.

Two women were walking down the narrow road. Their faces had an odd, unexpected familiarity.

"Excuse me," said Jade.

They ignored her and kept walking.

From the other direction, two more people approached.

Jade went over to them. "Could you please tell me when the train leaves for India?"

They ignored her too. They didn't so much as slow down to look at her.

Jade sighed. Not exactly a friendly place.

Finally she bumped into two more people. Jade used a feigned stumble as an excuse to take one of them gently by the arm. She pointed to the train and asked, "When does the train leave?"

The person shook their head, and their companion pulled them away from Jade. They walked quickly.

At least they knew she was there.

The companion spoke, though. Finally, someone said something to her. It was as they walked away, but still, it was something—

Jade stood frozen. It didn't make any sense. She must not have heard them well. Or her translation skills must be faulty.

But what the hell could they mean when they said, "What train? It's been years since a train last passed through here."

Jade turned and looked again. The train was right there.

Was she the only person who could see it?

It didn't take long to wander through the little village. Jade hoped to find some little place that served food. A bowl of hot soup and steaming tea was what she needed. Those were the traveler's first remedies for tough situations. Jade had learned that long ago. Whenever the road was difficult, the best thing to do was to stop for a bit and get a hot meal, or at least a hot drink. It put the world in perspective, and often it could help you figure out what to do.

Nothing seemed open, though. Or little eating-places didn't exist here. Jade saw one place that looked promising, but the door wouldn't open. People inside wouldn't look at her, or open the door for her, or acknowledge her at all.

Jade gave up trying. There was only one more thing. The day was getting on. Sooner or later she would need to figure out a place to stay. A small building ahead had the look and feel of a hostel, so Jade made her way toward it.

She'd figure out a way to get a room, a bed, hell, a spot on the floor. She'd figure out a way to get word to The Management.

She stopped.

Did they already know?

What sort of awareness did they keep of their Jakes and Jades? Especially rookies who weren't where they should be? Did The Management know? Were they already mobilizing help?

Jade's eyes narrowed. Or had this strange abduction circumvented their knowledge? They might think Jade was where she should be. They might have no idea that she wasn't in India, but was wandering a small unfriendly village in Tibet?

Who could be powerful enough to hide not only a train but also this entire incident from The Management?

Jade started walking again, more determined now. The sun was dipping toward the western mountains. Already Jade could feel a chill in the air. She was ready to be inside, within the safety and comfort of four walls. She needed to think, to figure out what to do next.

One more alley to pass by, and she would be at the little hostel.

"One way or another," she said, "I'm going to get inside."

She stepped between the two buildings. The alley ran between them. A curious darkness, an unexpected shadow, spilled out toward Jade's feet.

A chill, not of the air, went through Jade. She stepped faster, ready to be away from the shadow.

Then something grabbed her, and pulled her into the alley.

5

ALLEY

During her training, the first time someone threw a punch at her, Jade fed them back their own knuckles.

Her conflict management and prevention instructors appreciated her reflexes. Nonetheless they also told her she had failed.

The second time she did better.

When the punch came, she stepped out of the way. Her opponent kept swinging at her. Jade dodged, sidestepped, or moved in a circle. By the time they circled the room a few times, her opponent was gasping and struggled to keep their hands up. Jade had hardly broken a sweat.

That time she passed.

The third time someone in training took a swing at her, she wasn't in a training room. A simple slight had flared up into a fight. Jade caught the person's hand and said the only thing she could think of that made sense.

"I'm sorry."

They wound up having a long chat, and got along much better from then on.

After that, her conflict instructors said she had learned all she needed from them.

Now, an unseen force pulled her into the dark alley. Jade didn't want to walk around a room. She sure as hell didn't plan to apologize for anything. Whatever was happening here, they were going to eat their own damn knuckles.

The strange force set her down, but before she could counter, it vanished. The alley felt empty and small, yet also somehow narrow and wide at the same time. The street was far behind her now, as if the alley were longer than it looked. Looking behind her, the end of the alley was a little rectangle of light. It seemed cramped enough that Jade almost felt claustrophobic. Yet when she moved from side to side, she could not find a wall.

Dimness gave way to mistiness. The air gained a soft flow, like fog falling through yellow streetlights. But there were no streetlights here. Nor fog. Only the arid air of a village at high elevation.

Jade tried to see through the darkness. "Who are you? Why did you bring me here?"

No answer.

Fists clenched, Jade slid her right foot back. She raised her arms, ready for the fight, the fury.

Then she lowered her arms and opened her hands.

This wasn't a fight. It was only her, standing alone in the dark.

If someone were trying to mug her, they wouldn't dally. If they meant her any other harm, there'd be no preamble.

Instead she remembered a simple thing that could improve most difficult situations.

"I'm listening," she said.

"We are glad to hear it, Jade Agamuskara Bluegold." The voice was disembodied yet solid. It seemed to come from three individuals all at once, yet also was the same voice, complete and unified.

Jade's eyes widened.

She hadn't seen them since the day she was chosen and had chosen. Once a Jake or Jade accepted their destiny, they often never saw them again.

But here they were. Before her.

The Management.

From the dimness, forms came out of the shadows. Three hooded figures stood before her. They floated. Or their long hooded robes obscured their feet. If they had feet. Jade had no idea, and if any fellow student or instructor had known, they didn't say. No one knew what The Management were: human or inhuman, mortal or god, good or evil.

The figure in gold and silver was in the middle. On its left was the figure in brown and black, and on its right was the figure in blue and green.

"You learned what was going on," said Jade. "Thank goodness. I didn't know how I was going to get word to you. I have so many questions, and I don't know the extent of what is going on around here."

The figure in gold and silver raised a hand. "We do,' said The Management.

"You do?"

The figure in blue and green came forward. "We brought you here."

Before Jade could say anything, the figure in brown and black came forward. "We need your help."

"My help?" Jade shook her head. "I thought I was already helping you. By starting my first job as a Jade, in Agamuskara."

"That will come," said The Management. "But not yet. This is more important. What do you know about the Heart of the World?"

"It's a legend," replied Jade. "A myth that travelers rhapsodize about after too much wine. People say it's a hidden horror, a place of cruelty, darkness, and depravity."

"The Heart of the World may be many things," said The Management, "but it is not a myth. It is real. And it is here. In Tibet. We know little of the Heart. It is a place beyond our purview and mission. We are... not welcome there. But we have been asked to help."

"Help? Help what?"

"The Heart of the World is under attack," said The Management. "The force responsible is something we do not understand, but it attacks with the force of a vast army. Whatever is behind the attack is cunning, intelligent, and driven. We cannot stand against this force, not in a direct fight. We do not know that anyone could. But we know what this force wants. Inside the Heart lies a great power. If unleashed, much harm will come. This force could wipe out life as we know it... or all life, for all time."

Jade tilted her head. "And whoever or whatever is attacking the Heart... wants to do this?"

"Yes. We do not know exactly where the Heart is. With the right guide you can go to the Heart of the World. We need you to stop the force trying to break in, and protect not only those who live in the Heart, but in all the world."

Jade said nothing. The enormity of it all washed through her. Go into an inhospitable landscape. Spend who knew how long trying to find a place that people didn't think existed. And then stop some sort of unknown but powerful son-of-a from trying to destroy the world.

"Why me?"

The three figures of The Management looked at each other, then back at Jade. "What do you mean?"

"I'm a rookie," said Jade. "There are more experienced Jakes and Jades."

"We chose you," said The Management, "because you are kind. When a thief tried to steal from you, you showed kindness and understanding. You gave him another chance."

"Are you saying that you want me to find a way to give this... evil being... some sort of second chance?"

"We are saying, Jade Agamuskara Bluegold, that you are the only one who has any chance." The Management paused, and their silence seemed like a sigh. "Either you can stop this, or no one can."

"I'm going to face great dangers," she said.

"Of course," said The Management. "No quest is without them."

"I might die."

"If you die," said The Management, "we all die. We know the task is great, but as you understand, so is the need. We need you, Jade. The world needs you. Do you accept?"

"You say that as if I have a choice."

"Of course you have a choice," said The Management. "You always have a choice. Choosing is only a matter of which consequences you can accept."

Jade stared at each of the three hooded figures. Definitely floating. No way they were actually touching the ground.

"No," said Jade. "There's no way I can do this. You've got to find someone else."

Without waiting for a reply, Jade left the alley and began running back toward the train station. The world was brighter outside the alley, though night was getting close. It'd be best to get back on the train. Wait for someone to show up. Anyone. As long as they could get her to Agamuskara. Or... well, Jakes and Jades were good learners. She didn't know how to drive a train. She smiled. But she knew she'd be a quick study.

Turning a corner, Jade came back to the main thoroughfare she had gone down earlier. She got back to the platform—and stopped.

The train was gone.

So were the ticket building and the tracks, and any other sign that a few hours ago a train had arrived here.

She turned. The Management were behind her, silent as they walked or floated or whatever the hell they did.

Jade's eyes narrowed. "Not much of a choice." Her voice was low and icy.

"We never said it would be," replied The Management. "Only that you had one."

"Am I still going to work in Agamuskara, at the Everest Base Camp?"

"Of course," said The Management. "As long as you survive."

"Fine," said Jade. "I accept. I'll find the Heart of the World. I'll confront this evil being... and I'll stop them, change them, thwart them... somehow. But bugger if I know how."

"Thank you, Jade," said The Management.

Jade held up a hand to cut them off. "I don't need anything else," she said. "The world is depending on me. If I fail, everything might die. I get it. The burden is on me, all that usual hero crap. Not saying I like it. I understand it, though, and I'll do it anyway."

"And that, Jade," said The Management, "is why we asked you. The hero was already there, ready to emerge."

"Only thing is," said Jade, "I have no idea where I'm going."

Footsteps crunched on the platform. Mim and Pim stepped out of the shadows and stood near Jade and The Management.

"We can show you the way to your next destination," said Mim.

"Fine," said Jade. "It's late, though, and I'm exhausted. Can I at least get a decent sleep first?"

"There's a place in the village where you may rest for a few hours," said Pim. "We'll take you there. Then we leave at dawn."

Jade turned to give one last look at The Management, but they were already gone.

With a sigh and a shake of her head, Jade left the platform and walked with the brothers into the gathering night, toward the place where she would sleep, wondering what strangeness would arrive when the new day came.

6

SCRATCH

When they got to the top of the cliff, Jade stopped and looked back. The village where she'd slept shimmered behind them in the morning light. Or seemed to. Jade looked more closely. Did it shimmer? Or did she one moment see the village, and another see nothing but bare rock, devoid of any sign of human habitation?

Mim and Pim stood on either side of her, and she looked from one to the other.

"Was it really there?" she asked.

Mim shrugged. "Is anything?"

"If I come back this way, will it reappear?"

Pim patted her shoulder. "The way is long," he said. "Think only of what is before you now."

"Oh yes," said Jade. "A joyful jaunty wander to the end of the world. All for an impossible mission where my failure means destroying the world. Not something a gal forgets."

They turned and again faced the direction they would be walking for the next few days. North, deeper into the mountains. Green gave way to brown. Brown gave way to white.

"It becomes so desolate," said Jade. Even though the eastern sun was shining on her right side, nothing in the world felt warm.

"Even in desolation, life can surprise you," said Mim.

He took a step but stumbled. Jade caught him, her hand on his chest.

Her brow furrowed. Something wasn't right. Before she could ask or comment, he straightened himself and stepped away from her. Pim followed, and Jade rushed to keep up.

Middle of nowhere. Two strange men. Sent by The Management or not, Jade didn't like anything about the situation.

"You know you can trust us," said Mim.

"I don't know anything," replied Jade.

"We are also assuming that we can trust you," added Pim.

"Trust me?"

Mim's eyes narrowed. "That's enough, Pim," said Mim.

The brothers went silent. For two hours they walked north. They said nothing. Now and again they glanced toward the sun as it rose into the bright bleak sky. They went between the folds of hills that one day would become mountains. They walked through small rifts and valleys. The sun became a memory overhead, the shadows deep and the air cool around them. They emerged in sunlight at the tops of hills. Over small plateaus their boots crunched over rocks and stubby grasses. The occasional yak, shaggy and black, would stare, as if wanting to ask why in the world people had ventured all the way out here.

Jade wished she understood the answer.

The second day brought them higher, deeper into the Himalayas. They trudged their way along a narrow, bumpy ledge that wrapped around a cliff. Coming around a bend in the face of the high cliff, Jade stared down to the bottom of the world. So far below—she tried not to let the dizziness overwhelm her. Above the world yet tethered to it. All that kept her going was a little narrow strip of rock. The ledge wound around the cliff up ahead, toward a destination unknown.

Her foot hit a rock, which skittered across the ledge and tumbled over. Jade lost sight of its descent, toward a river below. The waters gleamed, so bright teal they seemed painted, not part of a real landscape.

Jade held her breath. She tried not to think of the rock. Or how wide that river was. From so far up, though, the flowing water seemed like a thin ribbon.

Eyes closed a moment, Jade exhaled and took another step along the ledge.

She slipped.

She saw the rock again, its tumble toward the edge so slow, its fall toward the water so fast.

Her feet left the rock. There was no training now, no reflex, only a surrender to physics and gravity. Jakes and Jades could do many things—but they could not fly.

Jade fell. It felt like tears gathered in her eyes. Maybe she couldn't fly, but at least the rush of falling through the dry air was sending her tears into the sky. She stared down. When she died, would it be destiny thwarted or destiny achieved? She'd never know.

The ribbon of the river looked wider now—

She stopped.

Mim and Pim each held on to one of her arms. Together they pulled her back onto the ledge. Jade stood against the wall, pressing into it as if ready to dig a cave and hide inside. Her breath came fast in the thin air.

"That way's not for you, Bluegold," said Mim.

"I didn't expect this way to be for me either," replied Jade.

"Neither did we," said Pim. "Are you okay?"

"I'll get there," she said. "Thank you for saving me."

The brothers nodded, and they kept going. Finally they emerged from the cliff and its little ledge. The chasm faded behind them, and the ground was level and unbroken again. Jade ran forward onto a flat expanse of sun-yellowed rock. There was warmth here, and so much light. Jade reveled in the heat on her face and hands.

"Come over here," she called to her companions as she sat down in the sun. "Warm yourselves up a little before we go on."

Mim and Pim sighed. They came over to her. Though Jade felt ready to have a nap, they didn't seem to even be breathing hard. Sweat covered her body, but they looked as dry as the air and the dusty hills.

"A short rest does sound wise," said Mim, sitting down across from Jade.

"What's wrong?" Jade shook her head. "You look uncomfortable."

"This is all so strange for us," said Pim.

"We usually don't work in such a straightforward manner," said Mim.

"Do you work for The Management?"

"No," said Pim. "We're what you might think of as... freelancers. We have allegiances. We have obligations. But we don't serve any one being or any one force."

"You've scratched the skin, though," said Jade.

Mim shook his head. "Scratched the skin?"

"That's how I've always thought about it," said Jade. "Ever since The Management first appeared to me and offered me the choice of becoming a Jade."

Jade traced her finger over the thin soil. "This world, it's like it has this thin skin over it. That's most people's lives, the usual things that seem like the entirety of our existence. Our jobs, families, friends, the little obligations we must tend to as people. It's the grocery stores and the walks down the street. It's all everyday, ordinary, nothing to see here."

Jade scratched the ground deeper. "Sometimes, though, something happens to you. An encounter, a moment—you see something people aren't meant to see. One instant tells you the truth: What little you've known of the world is a thin skin. A mask covering the reality beneath. The cover is all so beaten up, so worn down, so threadbare. It's easy to think that's all the world. But in those rare moments, you can scratch through the skin. You can go through the covering—and see something else. Behind all that gray dustiness, there's something shining underneath."

Mim and Pim nodded. "That's one way to look at it," said Mim.

Jade stopped scratching at the dirt. "What's another?"

"People see what they want to see," said Pim. "There's nothing hidden, not really. Most things are in plain sight. People do an incredible job of refusing to see what's right in front of them. They ignore reality and then say it's what they search for. It's all right there. Before their very eyes and souls."

Mim shrugged. "The world can be what it is," he said. "It's up to people to decide whether they can accept that."

Jade lifted her finger from the rock.

"That spot wasn't a good illustration," said Pim.

The rock and dirt beneath was as bare and dusty underneath as it had been before she dug at it. Jade shrugged. "Trying to enhance the metaphor."

But she couldn't help but feel disappointed. She believed what she had said. Completely. She had seen behind things. Jakes and Jades were behind things, but they were one factor among many. There was The Management, but also other forces and powers. Jade still didn't know what half of them were. But once, just once, she wanted to scratch at the ground and see it actually shine.

She sighed and stood. Not today, though. "Let's keep going," she said.

They got up and walked on. Behind them, a little breeze tumbled over the hills. It puffed away more of the dirt from where Jade had been scratching at the skin of the world.

Underneath, glinting in the Tibetan sun, something shone.

7

DANCE

The start of their third day dawned slow and quiet with the rising sun. Shivering as she left her sleeping bag, Jade put it away and stared at the mountains surrounding them. The sun wasn't over them yet, and the night's chill lingered in the dim air. Jade brewed coffee over a fire. It was likely the last fire they would have for some time. Given the barrenness of the world ahead, firewood or any sort of fuel was likely to be in short supply.

The brothers were already up and had gone off somewhere. Jade looked at where they had slept the night before. Or, at least, where they had lain. Jade wasn't certain they slept. Overnight when she stirred to pick rocks out from under her back, she could sense the brothers. They were awake, as they had been each night. They didn't sleep. And what little they ate seemed to be more for show than for sustenance.

Then there was that matter of when her hand had touched Mim's chest, where his heart lay—

A pounding beat pulsed through the ground.

Jade jumped to her feet. She looked all around, from the ground before her, up the slopes of the mountains. She saw no one. All was still—

A rumble broke the world.

Training and panic fought one another, but the training won out. Jade leaped to one side and rolled along the dusty, pebbly ground. Sitting up, a boulder the size of a car had flattened the campfire.

So much for coffee.

More rumbles broke out. The hillsides had come alive. Rocks danced all over the slopes, bashing each other then tumbling into the trio's hollow.

Jade looked all around. Rocks were tumbling down behind her, the way they had come last night when they chose this spot for their camp. Some were starting down the mountainsides now, close, too close to her—

Jade ran forward. She passed the fire-flattening rock and dodged around another rolling boulder. Glancing at the mountainsides out of the corners of her eyes, a stretch seemed like it was calm. Or at least absent of falling rocks. She turned and started up the slope. If she could get to high ground, then it would be all right. She could hear only the roars of rocks colliding, breaking, tumbling, and falling. Now and again there was something different in the sounds, but she couldn't make it out.

Jade was halfway up the slope when the ground shook again. The vibration messed up her footing, and Jade tripped over a stone jutting from the ground. She smacked the earth hard, and it knocked the wind from her. Wheezing, trying to move, Jade looked up. A rock had come loose above her, and it gained momentum as it rolled toward her. She coughed and struggled to her knees, but more coughing made her stumble over again.

The rock was closer now. Too close. There was no getting away now.

Jade's eyes narrowed. No way she was dying here, under a damn rock.

She forced air into her shocked lungs. She tensed, made her body find its strength. And she leaped.

The rock rolled on by, crashing down the slope to smack into other large rocks below.

The sound was there again. This time it was more distinct, forcing itself beyond the cacophony of stone. She looked around, trying to find the source, but at least she could finally understand it.

A voice. Calling her name.

She tried to look up, to see something other than the rock.

Down below, boulders and piles of rubble surrounded Mim and Pim on all sides. They had one little space where they should be able to get away and start up the slope.

Except they couldn't.

Pim was dragging Mim. Mim must have fallen, or a rock must have hit him. He didn't look like he could stand.

Jade yelled, "I'm coming!" She ran toward them, angling down and across the slope, dodging rocks with every step.

The ground leveled out and Jade stood before them.

"We'd gone to check the way ahead," said Pim. He was trying to hold up Mim, who wasn't sweating but looked clammy. "When we got back, a rock came down and hit Mim. He can't make it out like this."

Jade went to Mim's other side and pulled him up, putting his arm across her neck. "Together we can get him out," she said.

"But the rocks," said Pim.

Jade shook her head. "I know the way."

They went up, as steadily and quickly as they could. Jade could see it now, could follow the rocks and read their paths. She could anticipate when one was about to come loose, and where it was going to go. Cutting around a bouncing rock, the three of them finally came far enough up the slope that they could sit down. Pim set down Mim. Mim grabbed his leg. Jade could see from his tensed face that he was trying to hold back screams despite tremendous pain.

Jade studied his leg. "Is it broken?"

Mim shook his head. "Leave me be." His voice was quiet but strained. "It's not as bad as it looks."

Pim stared at Jade. "Thank you," said Pim. "Without you, we wouldn't have gotten out of there."

The world went silent again. The rocks stopped falling. The ground stopped heaving.

Jade stared out over the changed landscape, where minutes ago they had their simple camp. The space between mountains was now a field of rubble. Their way forward was gone too. What had been a narrow but passable way was now clogged with rocks and rubble.

"What the hell happened?" said Jade. "Was that an earthquake?"

Mim shook his head, too fatigued to speak anymore.

"The force attacking the Heart of the World," said Pim. "That force is using great power. Whatever is happening at the Heart is being felt here."

Jade felt the blood drain from her face. Her heart, which had been beating so quickly, paused. The world had been so warm— from the rising sun, from the exertion and rush of the danger. Now the Himalayas felt as cold as midnight.

"And this is what The Management think I can do something about?" She shook her head. "I barely got out of there. Barely could help you."

"You did, though," said Pim.

Mim nodded.

"I can't imagine how I'm going to stop this… force. This evil," said Jade.

Mim patted her shoulder. "Start with being glad you are alive." He lay down his head and closed his eyes.

Jade stared at him. "Uh, Pim? Should we be letting him do that? If he's got a broken leg, there's shock—"

"He'll be okay," said Pim. Pim touched his brother's face and shrugged. "He just needs a rest."

"Are you sure that's all he needs?" said Jade. "I mean, should we go back, find him a doctor?"

"Your duty is far more important." Pim shook his head. "Besides, what doctor do you think is around here? Yaks don't have medical degrees."

Jade looked at Mim's sleeping form. She watched his chest. Waited for what she didn't expect to see. And wasn't surprised when it didn't happen.

"Pim?"

He followed her gaze to his brother's chest.

"It's not what you think," he said.

"And what do you think I think?"

"That we're not alive," said Pim.

"Are you?"

He shrugged. "Yes. And no. We are... between."

Jade leaned back. "I won't insult you by implying you're zombies."

"Such an overused device in stories, yet you don't exactly have another way to think about it," said Pim. "I understand. We are not exactly something you encounter every day." He grinned. "Then again you could, only you don't realize it. That's part of the fun. So many times we pass people and they think they recognize us. You can see it in the stutters in their voices, the pauses and stumbles in speech, step, breath. We're all over the place, Jade, doing many things. Some are for The Management. Some are for... another we serve."

"Who do you serve?"

"Our first rule is that we never say who we serve."

"Of course it is," said Jade.

"Something happened to us, long ago," said Pim. "But we could not pass on. Not yet. There was more for us to do here. We exist, but we do not live in the way you do. That is why we saved you. That is why we are so adamant that you do what you must to stop the force from doing what they are doing to the Heart of the World."

"Because death is so terrible?"

"Death is not terrible," said Pim. "Death is like walking, only you take one step in life and take the next step in death. It's part of the journey, Bluegold. What's terrible is knowing how precious life is, because you do not fully have it anymore, and then seeing how carelessly people treat it."

"Why do you call me Bluegold?"

Pim snorted. "One day, you'll know. But it's not for me to say."

"I want to know."

"Sometimes what you want is not what you need," said Pim. "This is one of those times."

"But I want to be in Agamuskara. I chose and was chosen," said Jade.

"Yet what you need to be is here," said Pim. "Going on this journey, toward an enemy you think is impossible to defeat. The Management aren't interested in sending you off to sacrifice your‐self. It would only make things worse anyway. The Management want you to save the world. They believe you are the only one who can."

"But why?"

Pim shrugged. He tried to make his gaze cold, but his eyes said he knew more than he could say. "That's not what matters right now," he said instead. "They made their choice. The trouble is, you haven't. You want to be a Jade of the Jakes and Jades? You want to see this quest through and have the best chance of saving not only yourself but the world? The Management believe in you. Mim and I believe in you. It's time you did too."

With a sad, resigned smile, Pim said nothing else. He turned away so he could stare at the sun and keep an eye on his brother. Jade tried to get him to say more, but Pim wouldn't look at her. He sat there, still and silent, looking at the sun so intently Jade wondered if he were somehow talking with it.

Jade sighed. She thought back over the training. Over all her years before she met The Management. That life hardly seemed like a life: Breaking away from where she had grown up. Wandering the world. Landing in Hong Kong, meeting Declan. Then the day he asked her a question, but she said yes to someone else's.

It had all brought her here. Sitting on a Tibetan hillside, surrounded by mountains. Feeling thin, warmish sunlight. Dry air and low oxygen making her throat as scratchy as a yak's arse. Oh, and she had nearly died in a rockslide caused by some unknown evil that was only just now warming up.

She didn't know what to say either.

The world was silent. The sun rose higher in the sky with not so much as a note or a word or a rasp.

Until Mim opened his eyes. He shot up from the ground, stood on his sturdy two legs, and began to whoop and whoop and whoop with joy.

Pim stood too, grabbing his brother's hands and leaping along.

Jade looked from one to the other. "What the hell are you doing?"

Mim paused and held out his hand to her. "Always be glad to be alive!" he said. "Life is all you've got. Make the most of every moment."

"But... this?" said Jade. "You're... capering."

"Of course," replied Pim, holding out his hand too. "The rocks came for us, but we survived. Our unknown enemy tried to kill us —though I doubt they knew it. Still, they tried to take us down, stop us from getting you on your way, and they failed. We live. We keep going. So of course we shout and dance!"

The smile came from Jade before she even realized it was happening. She let Mim and Pim pull her off the ground. They all took hands. Jade threw her head back and whooped and shouted. She called up all of the joy she knew to the sky and the wind and the clouds, to the mountains and the earth, to the faraway sea.

After a while, their hands fell away. Blood pounded through Jade's body. Her breath was fast, both from dancing around and from trying to take in more oxygen from the thin air. Puffs of brown-red dust made little clouds as they came off her coat and pants. With a nod they understood that it was time to get going again.

8

CLIFF

Jade led them down the slope to see what gear they could salvage, but the rocks had destroyed everything. All that remained of their beers was dark patches and twinkling shards on the thirsty earth. In the crushed ruins of their camp, they could find only Jade's backpack. Wedged under a rock, they pulled it free.

Jade expected the backpack to be soggy. There hadn't been much left in there, except for a little food, some extra clothes, and her last two bottles of GPS. Yet the rock had somehow missed the pack. Even the bottles were intact. Jade grinned.

"Granted, these beers will be the tastiest we've ever had," said Jade as she put on her pack, "but what will we do for food? What I have in here won't last long."

"We'll manage," said Mim.

"There are some plants that we can eat," said Pim. "We'll show you."

They set off. Cresting a hill, Jade paused and stared at the sky. Some clouds floated by here and there. One cloud, tall and broad and big as a mountain, passed them. It too headed north. As it passed, Mim and Pim glanced at each other and nodded.

"Let's keep going," said Mim. "There's a place we want to get you to. It will be much better—and should be much safer—for passing the night."

From the barren brown of the hills and rocks, they passed the next hours in a world that became greener. The air took on a refreshing coolness, not from the mountain air, but from the river lolling through a small, cliff-ringed valley. The world took on the freshness of running water—and of growing plants. The lush valley bottom was narrow but verdant. Mim and Pim showed her plants with leaves she could eat, roots she could cook. There was even an apple tree, heavy with ripe fruit.

"Now this is a pleasant surprise," said Jade. She plucked an apple and delighted in its crunch and tart sweetness.

"Get all you can," said Mim. "The going gets harder from here."

Jade sighed. "You could have told me that after I'd had a chance to enjoy this place, you know."

Mim shrugged and walked away.

Pim patted her on the shoulder. "You have so much ahead of you," said Pim. "This quest. And more. I don't know you as well as I should like, Jade Agamuskara Bluegold. One day I hope to. Even if you don't know it's where you needed to be, you'll always get where you need to go."

Mouth stuffed with apple, Jade couldn't reply. Pim looked her in the eye for a long time, though. Then, with that sadness in his gaze again, he walked away too.

Jade ate more apple and looked around. On the western side of the valley, a high cliff rose. It was so tall that someone standing on top could touch the sun as it passed over the roof of the world. Indeed, the sun was passing over the edge now. Jade wondered what it would feel like to stand there and feel the sun's nearness as it went by. The rock of the cliff face was black and almost shone in the light.

"Look at this cliff!" she shouted. "You guys, you have to see this."

The gurgles and rushes of the river replied, but the brothers did not.

"Mim? Pim?"

Jade searched the little valley, calling for her companions. But Mim and Pim were gone.

"No goodbye?" said Jade.

Tears stung her eyes with a cocktail of sadness, fear, and frustration. Mim and Pim were annoying yet endearing, and she'd grown to like them, their deep sadness and their joy, despite their belief in her. Now they'd vanished. She thought back to that nod as the cloud passed.

And she understood. They'd planned to do this all along.

Leave her stranded and alone, in the middle of the Himalayas. No guide. No map. No way to know which way to go.

Movement turned her gaze upward.

A figure stood at the edge of the cliff. Dark in black shadow and unseeable in the path of the sunlight, the figure raised its arms. Its hands wrapped around the sides of the sun. Jade started to call out, but she stopped. She didn't know who it was. Was it Mim and Pim, going up without telling her, to spy out the surrounding land? Had the force they sought sensed their presence—and now it had come to confront its enemies?

The figure seemed to bend its knees.

Then it jumped.

Jade took a step backward. Before she could stop herself, she yelled.

The figure turned toward her, must have looked straight at her.

Then it fell.

The world went silent. Until the thud.

9

VIGIL

The silence moved back in, desperate to fill in the void left by the fall.

Jade's mouth hung open. The chilling air dried up her throat. No voice, no words, no anything. A horrible silence followed the sound of the figure crashing into the ground.

Then she ran toward the grove where the shadowy figure had fallen.

"I'm not some idiot who gets to stand around slack-jawed," she said, fighting through the panic and the fear. "I'm Jade. I'm a Jade. I'm Jade. I'm a Jade."

The trees were taller than she was, but only by a few feet. Still, they were tall enough and the little grove thick enough to make it hard to move.

She cupped her hands around her mouth. "Hello! Where are you? Can you speak? I'm coming. I'll help..." She paused, not sure what the hell she could do. No medical gear. No doctors. Middle of nowhere. "I'll do what I can, anyway," she said in a smaller voice. "If I ever figure out what that is."

She fought her way over and through a bit of undergrowth. In the midst of the green, a dark shadow lay sprawled on the ground.

Plunging through the trees had torn the shadow's clothes. A lower leg jutted out at an angle that made Jade's stomach flip and churn. From tears and lacerations all over the person, blood trickled onto the earth.

Not the person. Jade shook her head.

Person implied life and living.

Body. The body on the ground. The body bleeding. The body, so still, and still not moving.

Jade swallowed and forced her stomach to stay in place. She made herself kneel next to the body. With gentle hands she touched the limbs and torso, trying to understand the extent of the damage. Her compassion fought against her stomach and her own sense of dread and horror.

"I'm sorry," she said. "It's my fault." Then she shook her head. "But no... It's not..."

She moved some brush aside, snapping plant stems and branches. At last she saw the man's face. Bald head. Skin the same reddish-brown as the Tibetan earth surrounding them. Wide eyes, as if in those last moments they had tried to see as much of the world as they could. Even in the gathering dark, the brown and black eyes gleamed. In life they must have been vivid. Now they stared up at a sky that soon would darken, but still would never be as dark as those eyes were now.

Tears pulled at Jade's eyes. Why had this happened? Why had he jumped in the first place? What sadness, horror, or hopelessness had, so literally, taken him over the edge?

Jade touched the face. The skin was still warm, but in the cooling mountain air she knew that wouldn't last long.

Whatever had happened on the way down, the dead man had managed to turn so he faced the sky. Had it been a hope of seeing some world beyond? Was he looking into some place beyond this one? Did it make it easier to step from this life to the next?

The tears came then, but not only for the death of the person before her. Tears poured down, hot and blazing. Jade looked to the sky as well, shouting and yelling until she was hoarse. She screamed at The Management for bringing her all this way. She roared at Mim and Pim for abandoning her—and at the worst moment, when now more than ever she needed help. She needed someone else to be with her, so she didn't have to deal with this alone. And she roared at herself. For saying yes to the wrong question. For not considering anything else. For thinking only of herself.

"There's nothing I can do for you." Jade shook her head and gazed at the body. "I should go. I have this quest. You're not part of it. Or if you were, then I guess I'm buggered now." Her hand flew to her mouth and her eyes widened.

"I'm sorry," said Jade. "I shouldn't have said that. Respect for the dead and all." She touched his left hand—and pulled back. It wasn't skin.

Jade looked down. A black leather glove covered the body's left hand, but the right hand was bare. The other glove must have come off in the fall somehow. Staring closer, Jade realized that while the right hand looked strong and whole, the left hand seemed smaller, and slightly misshapen. Maybe the presence of a single glove was deliberate after all, the remnant of some old, unhealed injury. Jade took the gloved hand in her own two hands and squeezed it.

"I wish I had been here sooner," she said. "I would have seen you. I would have come up there. We could have talked. I could have helped you. Instead of you jumping, we could have walked away from that cliff together."

The body's dark eyes stared at the sky. Jade checked again. For a pulse. A breath. Any sign of life. The body gave her none.

Jade looked away. Tears fell onto the ground. She looked up again. With a careful hand she closed the dead man's eyes.

Beyond the little grove, the quest waited. Jade started to rise. Then lowered back down.

She stared at the dead man's face. "It's not right to leave you, as if your death didn't matter," she said. "There is one thing I can do. My guides abandoned me here. You died, and I could do nothing to save you. I'm sorry for that. I can't change what happened. I don't know your name, or where you came from, or who might be wondering where you are. I don't know your life, your choices, your actions, or their consequences. But I'm here. If no one else in the world knows your fate, at least I do. In many cultures, someone stays with the dead for a time. Keeps their body safe. Makes sure the soul can pass on to, well, to whatever is next. I guess you'd know better than I do."

Jade shook her head and couldn't help but chuckle.

"I'm talking to a dead man," she said. She shrugged. "And why not?" She patted the dead man's hand.

"I'll stay with you. Sometimes simply being there is the best way to help. Well, I'm here. Whoever you were, wherever you are now. Please know that someone knew. Someone saw. Someone cared. I'll hold vigil with you, through the night, until the sun rises. Once you've gone on your way, I'll go on my way too."

The sun dipped beyond the cliff, and the little valley grew dark. Jade gathered some edible plants, along with some she could burn. She lit a fire and kept it fed. The air's chill fled before the flames, but it didn't go far.

Food didn't sound good, though. The dead man couldn't eat anymore. She shrugged. Fasting might as well be part of the vigil. Jade tucked the food into her backpack for the trip onward. Better to go hungry today to eat tomorrow. Odds were there wouldn't be another lush valley.

She sat in silence, gazing at the dead man. Night's shadows had overtaken him. The firelight flickered on the still face, but with reluctance, as if unwilling to dance on the dead.

"I've known grief," said Jade at last, to the clear moonless sky, to the stars filling the world above. She wondered if the man's soul was one of them now. "I've known sorrow and loss." The man was dead. She could say it. Here. In this place. To ears that heard no more.

"I left when I was a teenager," she said. "Not home. It doesn't deserve the honor of the name home. Everyone comes from somewhere, and that happened to be where I came from. It was too difficult to live with anymore. Any longer, and I... I would have made the same choice you did. I wish I could tell you someone intervened. Showed me how things could be better. How I deserved better. But no one did. I had to do this. All this. I had to go my own way, when I didn't even know what that meant." Tears stung her eyes again. "I don't know if you have family, or if you wish you did. I don't know what despair drove you to this. But I wish someone could have told you it could be otherwise. I wish you could have found that hope in yourself."

The lonely years washed over her, wandering the world with nothing but a little backpack. And the moment that had given her a chance to leave. A relative's faraway death had forced her parents to get her a passport. After they returned from the funeral, Jade knew they would burn it. So she took it and left before they could. She still remembered the woman who had let her onto the ferry. A little light of kindness had gleamed in her dark eyes. Jade knew that the woman knew that she was a minor. She should have turned Jade away. To this day, Jade didn't know what would have happened if she had. Jade wished, sometimes, that she could find that woman, if only to tell her thanks.

"I don't know what I'd be like now. That relative's death gave me a new life," said Jade. "Funny thing is, I'd never met them." She shook her head. "I'm supposed to be this great person, in charge of destiny and decision. The weight of the world will be on me more times than I can count. But I'm scared. I'm so scared. I have no idea if I can do this or not. If this is all there is for me. If this is who I am and what my life will be. I left someone behind, and it burns at me every day. I hope I can see this through. Some-times I don't know if I made the right choice. How am I supposed to guide people's destinies and decisions when I have so many doubts about my own?"

The dead man's face stared at the sky and remained silent. Jade thought he would have looked more placid, in the dark, in death, but it was as if there was a tension in his face. Even in death, the agonies and obligations of his life refused to let go.

The night sauntered darkly on, while Jade sat there and held his gloved hand. A few times she came close to dozing off, and she jerked herself awake. "I'm sorry," she said each time, hoping he would understand.

Sometimes she thought about leaving. The fire burned down and she let it die. It was time. No more light. Only the darkness. She hoped the dead man now had all the light he would need. It was time to let the body fade, let the cold and the insects and the microbes do their job.

But Jade didn't leave.

"I'll stay with you," she told him again, her little gleam of a mantra the only warmth and light in the dark and cold. "No matter the life, a person has died," Jade said. "I have to stay. Someone has to. It happens to be me."

Through the darkest, coldest long hours of the night, Jade shivered. She pulled on all her clothes to help keep her warm. It helped some, but she longed for the barest scrap of daylight. She wanted to run out of the valley and up onto a hilltop. She was ready to watch the sun slice open the sky and start moving across the new day. She wanted that warmth on her face. She could only hope that it would go deeper now, down into her heart and bones again, after this cold night with the dead.

Except for Jade's breathing, all was silent.

Then a little chitter sawed its way through the dark.

Some random insect sensed something Jade did not, and gave its own little good morning. There was no sun yet. But a little bird made a chirp. Another insect stirred. Somewhere nearby came a small rustle.

Jade too began to sense the change coming in the world. Even this night, this long cold night, was ending. Even in the darkness of death, there would be a new day, for a world that kept turning and moving. All the world had stopped for one person's death, but all the world kept going on too. Jade wondered how people managed to do both at the same time. How they hold the stillness and sorrow of loss. Yet all the while continued trying to keep up with life's ceaseless momentum.

With the coming light, though, would come the end of the vigil. Jade could feel it now. A little charge in the air. Not warmth, but the promise of warmth. It buzzed at her, electric and pulling, like a kiss in the final heartbeat before the lips touched.

Jade squeezed the dead man's hand one last time, one last measure of kindness and comfort.

"I must continue my quest," she said. "The world is in trouble. I have to help, although I don't yet know how. Whatever happened to you, whatever drove you to this choice, you had life, and it was worth something. Worth more than I can know or say. I'm sorry things ended this way. But please know this: I will remember you. I will carry you with me. As I do what I must do, I will think of you, your solitude, your loneliness. I will remember them as my own. I will use them to do all I can to those who need my help."

Jade patted the dead man's gloved left hand, then laid it on his chest. She folded the bare right hand over it, the skin still rich and supple. He must have been so strong in life. His body was broad, not beefy but sinewy, as if strength itself had taken form and become his flesh.

Leaning forward, Jade kissed the dead man's forehead.

"I will remember you," she said. "May your journey be calm and untroubled. May whatever is next be better than what came before."

Tears burned at her eyes again, but Jade made herself stand. Her body creaked, sore from the long stillness, but it was time to go. Time to leave the calm safe valley. Time to figure out wherever the hell she needed to go find the Heart of the World.

Jade sighed. "North," she said, feeling the world change, feeling the first glint of sunlight about to arrive. "That's about all I know." She shrugged. "I guess that's what I'll keep doing."

She took a step—then stopped when a hand grabbed her wrist.

10

BLOODY

"Bugger," said the dead man. "I was certain it was going to work that time."

Night's chill lingered, but the black leather wrapped around Jade's wrist was warm. The dead man sat up. His eyes were open again, the same deep brown and black. The faraway glassiness was gone. Now his gaze was on fire. Jade could all but see the flames burning behind the dark iris and the void of his pupil. As she looked, the little scratches on his face all healed up and vanished, as if they had never been there.

Yanking her wrist up and back, Jade freed herself. She turned as the adrenaline poured through her. North was all that mattered. Awake or not, the dead man's leg had broken in the fall. Outrunning him wouldn't exactly be a problem. Jade took a deep breath, swung back her arms, and bent forward a little, ready to break into a sprint.

But he was alive.

He was healing right before her eyes.

She unfolded her body, relaxed her arms and legs. Adrenaline spiked her blood. Her heart's pounding crashed like the boulders that fell the day before. Her mind told her to flee, but her training —and her heart—told her to stay.

Jade made herself turn and face him.

The air changed again, and a lightness came over the world. Above them, past the eastern top edge of the valley, an orange glimmer of sun emerged. A little ray of light came down to the little oasis. It landed between them at first, then spread, filling out over Jade's face and the dead man's face.

Jade took a step toward him.

She stumbled and fell forward. A jutting branch slashed her across the right cheek from lip to temple. Eyes widening in surprise as she recovered and stood, Jade raised her hand and wiped her cheek. It came away bloody.

Jade narrowed her eyes and locked her gaze on the dead man. She wiped the blood on her pants and waited.

11

THE PRICE OF BEING DIFFERENT

"Well, call me an eejit and steal my pint o' stout," said the dead man. He kicked his legs up, bent his body upward, and with a whoosh of air was on his feet. "You heal too."

Jade nodded. "It's a... benefit," she said.

"O' what?"

Jade's eyes narrowed. The man's face seemed like he should be from somewhere in this region: Tibet, northern India, Nepal, the Himalayas. But his accent was a deep thick Irish. He had jumped off a cliff. He had fallen. He had died, or at least he had done a damn good impression of it. Now he lived—and he healed like she could. Or even better. She didn't think a Jake or Jade could have survived that fall. Thought after thought swirled in her mind. Despite the maelstrom of confusion, these thoughts began to cling together. One by one they connected and formed a clear picture.

The Management had sent her here. Mim and Pim had guided her—not to the Heart of the World, as she had assumed they had agreed to do. But to her next destination.

Here. Where this man would be.

This was the moment. This was the person.

The guide who would take her to the Heart of the World.

How else was he connected to all this, though? How much could she trust him, whoever he was?

But to earn trust, Jade remembered, you had to risk giving trust in return.

So she decided. "Healing—along with not aging, and a few other attributes big and small—is a benefit of what I do and who I am," she said. "I'm a Jade of the Jakes and Jades. I'm supposed to be in India, starting my first job. But The Management sent me here on a special quest, a journey." She took a deep breath, and plunged on. "To find you. And to stop something that threatens all life."

The man's eyes narrowed. "Jakes and Jades? The Management?" His "th" sounded like a simple "t." "Never heard o' them."

Jade shrugged. "Yes you have."

"What makes you think that?"

"Because everything you've said was true. Until now."

"Can you always tell when someone is lying?"

Jade shook her head. "People are too complex for that. Situations and understandings are too multifaceted, based on too many factors. But often we can tell the difference between truth and not."

The man's lips curled into a half-smile. "Fine," he replied. "I'm aware o' The Management."

"And?"

He shrugged. "Another story for another time, lass."

Jade stared at him, but he wasn't going to say anything more. Not now. Instead of pushing him, she changed direction. "What did you think was going to work?"

"What?"

"When you came to. You said you thought it was going to work this time. Have you tried to kill yourself before?"

"Kill myself?" The man laughed. "That's the last thing on my mind. Horrible thing to do." The man looked up to the top of the cliff. "I wasn't trying to fall." He smiled. "I was trying to fly."

"Fly?"

He nodded. "And I was certain I'd gotten it right this time. I used to be able to fly. Then... something happened. I lost the ability. So I came here a while back. This area is where I learned to fly when I was a boy. I thought being here would help me get it back. Thing is, I was sure I'd done it. There's a lightness, you see. Not just o' the body, but o' the heart. The key to flying is that no matter what is happening in the world—or *to* the world—you must find a light heart. That's hard for me nowadays. But I thought I had, Jade. I thought I had. I was certain I could feel the lightness again."

She saw it in her mind again. The dark figure leaping. For a moment, he had hovered. "I'm sorry," she said. "My... yell... might have distracted you." Guilt flooded her. "It was a bit of a surprise."

The man shrugged. "It might have done." He chuckled. "But no harm done. Though I'm sorry for my own surprise. Most bangs and bonks aren't a big deal to heal from, but I needed some downtime, given the extent o' these injuries. Still, it's nothing compared to the hundred years I had to sleep after The Blast."

Jade's mouth opened. "The Blast? You were there?"

The man nodded. "At the epicenter. The injuries... the horror... I failed to stop it. I tried... but I couldn't. To this day I still don't know what happened."

Now she understood. The agony and obligation that had lined his face overnight, even in what seemed like death.

"I woke about thirty-five years ago," said the man. "Ever since then, I've been trying to find my place in this changed world. I do all I can to right the wrongs o' that horrible failure."

"Oh my goddess," said Jade. "You're him. You're Faddah Rucksack."

"Rucksack will suffice."

"I heard about you. During my decade training to be a Jade. You were... a whisper in the hallways. A story in the dark. Everyone said The Management refused to talk about you. They encouraged rumors that you were a myth. But you're real. A ten-thousand-year-old hero. A demigod."

"Like I said, Rucksack will suffice."

"Then after The Blast you vanished, and no one has heard anything about you since. The Management said only that there was a being that had lost its destiny, and we should fear it." Jade's eyes darkened. "They meant you."

Rucksack nodded. "The price I pay is high," he said. "But it's the same as yours."

"The price of what?"

"The price o' being different," said Rucksack, "is being apart. Existing apart. We do not, cannot, live in the normal world, amongst people with everyday lives. Some call 'em hohums. They just... live. But not us. We are fringe people. We live on the shadows. We protect life and existence. We guide decision and destiny, while in many ways sacrificing our own. It's a hard price, and it has cost me more than I ever knew it could."

From the dark eyes came not a fire now, but a glow, desolate and alone, a small gleam in a vast darkness. "But it's one I'll gladly pay. I love this world and all in it, and I will do all I can to protect it."

The sun rose higher over the valley, warming the world around them. Even Jade's face, skin, and bones felt the long dark chill loosen and fade. Jade's mind sped as she made sense of everything Rucksack had said. There was more to Rucksack than she had ever imagined. The Management wouldn't confirm or deny anything about Rucksack. Other rumors also went around where the Jakes and Jades trained. But it wasn't time for those questions. It was time for something else.

"Let's at least introduce ourselves properly," she said, holding out her hand. "Jade Agamuskara Bluegold."

"Faddah Rucksack." He shook her hand. In his grip she could feel both his gentleness and his immense power.

Jade let go. "Is it true that you only drink stout?"

"O' course," he replied. "My parents invented it."

"Your parents were the First Brewers?"

"Aye, but there's not exactly a pub out here."

Jade grinned, pulled off her backpack, and opened it. "Why yes, there is."

She rifled through her pack and set the two bottles of GPS on the ground between them.

12

───────

SUNRISE BEER

Rucksack smiled. He twisted off the non-twist caps with his bare right hand. He didn't even wince.

Jade stuck out her lower lip and nodded. "Not bad."

One corner of Rucksack's mouth twitched up. "It gets easier with practice."

With a clink and a nod, they looked each other in the eye. "Sláinte," said each, before taking a long pull off their respective bottles.

There is beer. There is beer at the end of a long day. There is beer you have at celebrations. There is the cold one with friends or family, after hard work, a hot summer's day, a wedding, or a funeral.

Then there is beer at sunrise.

There is no beer like a perfectly cold beer after the chilliest time of night. Especially after you have left all you knew and thought you were going to know. After you have survived harsh environments and mortal peril. After you have stayed up all night with a man you thought was dead—only to see him revive and heal before your very eyes.

No beer will ever taste so good as that sunrise beer.

Jade's GPS tipped back not too cold. The stout's dry, bitter bite woke her up better than any alarm clock. A malty sweet top note prevented the hoppy bitterness from taking over. Yet the hops kept the sweetness from becoming vapid, one-dimensional, and hollow.

Stout is the night sky in a bottle. Some swear that the best stouts have a little gleam inside. If you look just right, some say, you can see a star's white gleam in the midst of the dark beer. Stout is reality in a glass. Stout sharpens your perspective. It helps you see what is real, what is potential, and what is the difference between the two. Stout is a pillow after a long day and a swift kick up the arse when you are indecisive. Stout inspires when you are weary, and its rough-plush comfort soothes when the world is not as it should be.

And this one beer, this impossible survivor, was the best beer that Jade had ever tasted.

Rucksack wiped his mouth with the back of his gloved left hand. "It's not bad," he said. "Though as far I'm concerned, GPS hasn't been the same since Guru Deep and his damned Deep Inc. took over First Call Brewing."

The bitterness in his voice was not from the hops.

"There were rumors that you are quite the thorn in the side to Guru Deep," replied Jade.

"I try," said Rucksack. "There's a connection between his family and The Blast, why it happened, why I failed to stop it. I have to find that connection. It's part o' the reason I wanted to learn to fly again. Figured that would be a useful skill."

"What was it like?"

Rucksack's face beamed brighter than the morning sun.

"Glorious," he said. "I told you about having a light heart. Flying is more than that. Flying is seeing everything as it is yet also how it could be. When you fly, it is as if you know what it is to be only soul and spirit, as if you have transformed your body. I always loved it. Went all over the world, helping where I could.

People used to say that when you heard a tiger's roar upon a rush o' air, all troubles were about to end."

"But no story mentions you," said Jade. "The legends the world over, the rumors were always that you were this great hero. You saved the world countless times. You not only stopped evil, you changed it. There are stories throughout time and from all cultures that have to be about you, only none mention you by name."

"That's not a mistake either," said Rucksack. "That's by design. The greatest hero is the one no one knows. I knew early on that I would exist apart. I loved life and the world. So I stay in the background. I watch. I see people live and grow and change and die. The world turns, both same and different with every day. I needed my own little secret smile. Preferred no one know that I was around, cleaning things up behind the scenes. It kept me focused. Kept me getting up myself."

"We would hear similar at our training," said Jade. "Ten years I spent, outside of time and space, learning how to be a Jade of the Jakes and Jades."

"You lot are part o' why I only drink stout," said Rucksack. "Don't want anyone mucking about with my decisions and destiny."

"But there's nothing to muck with," said Jade. "You don't have a destiny."

"I lost my destiny in The Blast," said Rucksack, his voice flat as old beer. "Whatever was going to happen to me that day, it's all gone. My life now is figuring out what I do instead, how I can still be useful in this scarred world."

"You've existed apart all this time," said Jade. "Ten thousand years."

"Oh, it's not as bad as all that," said Rucksack. "Mum, Dad, and I lived some long peaceful centuries in India, though that was long before India was India. Around where Agamuskara is now, in fact." He tipped his beer bottle toward her, then took another long pull off it. "We didn't hide, then. We coexisted. Our abilities were no secret. Over time people began to notice that none o' us grew old. Though their families died, we lived. Instead o' seeing that we cared, that we only wanted to help, people began to fear us. In time the fear overtook the people we lived near. One night, when the people's fear grew a thirst for our blood, we fled and didn't look back. After years o' wandering, we made our way to Ireland and lived there ever since. We figured out some good tricks to help us seem to age and change, and haven't had a problem again. Nowadays I hide in plain sight, and likely will as long as I live."

"You don't think there could come a day when people accept you as you are?" Jade shook her head and took another drink of stout. "It's been a long time."

"I long for that day," said Rucksack. "I yearn for that day to come. But I don't hope for it. Hope implies certainty, implies happening, as long as you hold true to luck and striving—and as long as they hold true to you. I can't let myself hold that day in my mind as some sort o' inevitable future tomorrow. I want it to happen but I don't think it will. I hold a desire, but a long time ago I let go o' the expectation that it will happen. If that day comes, I'll let it surprise me. For now, I don't give it any expectations. That goes a long way in preventing disappointment."

Jade stared at him, said nothing. She drank her beer and thought. There were so many things her fellow trainees used to say in the hallways. Rucksack was the ancient hero, the hero of old, the hero who had fallen and vanished. She didn't mention the rumors about the Hong Kong Incident, about all those people whose memories had to be changed as a result of whatever happened that day in Hong Kong. The Management refused to speak of it. They had even threatened Jakes and Jades with expulsion for looking into it too much. What happened in Hong Kong ten years ago still rattled The Management. Jade wondered if she was sitting across from a key person in the whole thing.

Now wasn't the time for that conversation, though. When she looked at Rucksack, she now and again sensed that he was holding back something too. It was almost as if he recognized her from somewhere, but was unsure where. Or didn't want to say so for some reason.

Jade thought hard about asking him. Seeing what the connection was.

Then there was the quest.

Already she had given too much time to this little valley. But that time had also yielded something of great importance: a new guide.

"I'm figuring I found you for a reason," said Jade.

Rucksack raised an eyebrow. "What would that be?"

"The Management brought me here because they said I was needed at the Heart of the World," Jade replied. "They couldn't take me there. Said they are not welcome."

Rucksack laughed. "No kidding they're not."

"You know the Heart?"

"O' course," said Rucksack. "You can find your way only if you don't know that you know the way. My mum grew up there. She left when she was young, because she wanted to see the world beyond the Heart. Caused no end o' grief for her parents."

"There are rumors about the Heart, you know," said Jade. "That it's full of cruelty and despair. The Heart of the World indeed."

"It's not." Rucksack shook his head. "It's like with me and my parents. People fear things they don't understand. When something is different, or beyond where they are, only the rare person sees wonder instead o' fear. The Heart is a place o' kindness and sense, o' peace, love, and striving. So many people think there is little else to life but cruelty and despair. The people o' the Heart thought otherwise, but could not convince others. They would rather live in a barren mountain than endure amongst so much pain and hurt. The Heart o' the World is not a place o' cruelty and despair, Jade. It's the respite—and the second chance. If cruelty and despair took over the world, the Heart is the one place that could restore life, hope, courage, and possibility."

"You sound like you know it well."

"I've been there many a time," said Rucksack. "The people o' the Heart are my family. My grandmother is the one who taught me to fly. She gave me lessons here, in this very valley. It was the only time in eons that she left the Heart."

"I have to go to the Heart," said Jade. "But I do not know the way. Will you guide me there?"

Rucksack opened his mouth, but stopped. A shadow fell over his eyes.

"No," he said. "I won't go back to the Heart o' the World."

"But it's your family. You know the way."

"I cannot go back there." He turned away and finished his beer. Then he stood. "I must get going. I need to resume my flying lessons. Guru Deep is up to something. If I'm going to mess up his operations in Moscow, I have a great deal to do. It was wonderful meeting you, Jade Agamuskara Bluegold."

He pointed north. "The way to the Heart is to keep going that way. Forget all that you think you know, and know only that the heart is what matters. Focus on that, and you will find your way."

"Please don't leave," said Jade. "Please help me."

"I cannot go there." He started walking away.

And Jade understood. "You're ashamed."

"What?" Rucksack stopped, his back to her, but he turned his head to look at Jade over his shoulder.

"The Blast," said Jade. "You couldn't stop it. You don't want to go there because you're ashamed and you don't know what they'll think of you."

"I told you how to get there." Rucksack's voice was flat and cold. "That's all you need."

"No it's not," said Jade. "I need help. The Management sent me because the Heart is under attack."

Despite the shadows over his face, Rucksack had gone pale. "Under attack? Is everyone okay?"

"I don't know," said Jade. "All I know is someone is trying to break in. Some great unstoppable evil. The Management have no way to stop it. They're terrified. They say that if this evil breaks in, there is a power they could use to destroy all life. They might wipe out everything in the world that you have dedicated your life to saving."

Rucksack stood there, silent, his eyes narrowed. But he didn't walk away either. Finally, slowly, he turned to face her again but said nothing.

"I stayed by your side when I thought you were dead," said Jade. She tried to keep her voice even, but a high pleading note broke through. "And if you help me, I... I will help you learn to fly again."

"Do you know how to fly?"

Jade shrugged. "No, but at the moment you don't either. You might be a wretched teacher... but how about we figure it out together?" She couldn't help but wonder what it would feel like to fly.

Rucksack nodded. "I suppose I do owe you," he said. "All right then. I'll guide you. Flying lessons be damned. The Heart o' the World is another week's trek."

"Another week?"

"You're lucky," said Rucksack. "Normally it'd be three. But you're tough." He grinned. "We can go the special way. It's also the hard way, but it will be faster."

He started walking. Jade hurried to keep up.

PART II

13

LESSON

Jade landed on her face. Again.

"Your heart is still too heavy," said Rucksack.

Leaning against a tree, he was trying not to chuckle—or at least trying to seem like he was trying not to chuckle.

Jade started to get up, but a flare of pain stopped her. Her shoulder had popped out of joint. She clamped her lips tight, but pain blazed through her arm, chest, and back. Teeth gritted, she waited for her healing to crunch the shoulder back into place. Then she got up.

Jade spat the dirt out of her mouth, but she hardly bothered to brush off the dust. By this point it was everywhere. She shifted her legs and hips and winced at the chafing.

Gods was it everywhere.

"This is what I get for relying on a teacher trying to teach me something he can't do himself," said Jade.

Rucksack shrugged. "Yet you continue the lessons."

He had her there. They'd been at it for hours. She would climb up a boulder, as tall as she was. She would leap—then fall. Usually she'd twist an ankle or dislocate a joint in the process. Jade sighed and climbed up the boulder again.

The midday sun warmed her and whisked away the sheen of sweat on her skin. Jade and Rucksack were at the edge of a slope, not too steep, at the bottom of which was a thin forest. Before them, beyond the trees, a strange beige plain unfolded. Brown barren hills ringed it on three sides.

After days of trekking, avoiding rockfalls, and enduring more quakes, Jade and Rucksack had found this place. On the way, the two of them had summited a few minor mountains, the world before them glorious in the sun. Though the tight lows passes had far outnumbered the high peaks, Jade shuddered at the thought of the narrow passages they'd barely scraped through. In places, the mountains crowded together so tightly, Jade and Rucksack had to turn sideways to pass between the high, narrow walls. In tight passages, the mountains stretched so high that the sky became a narrow blue strip. Now, after emerging from the final passage—and with scratches on both shoulders as tolls for the passing—the sky stretched edge to edge over the world. Jade breathed in and out deeply, so relieved to see that the sky was still broad and domed. Below them, and just beyond the slight forest, the flat plain stretched ahead too. The brown-red dirt lay barren—except for a scattered array of two dozen boulders.

"It's like a marbles board for goddesses and gods," said Jade.

"Not like," Rucksack said. "Is."

"Is?" said Jade. "It really is a game board?"

"What happened here happened long before my time," replied Rucksack. "It happened before my parents' time too, but my mother's people told a story about this place. If they were here, they would say that this is indeed a game board, only that right now there is no game being played. Some stories say these rocks are monsters, or old warriors, turned to stone, or a bit o' both. Some say deities and demigods moved the pieces; others say they were the pieces. But there's trouble with this game. All its turns and attempts, wins and losses, victories and destruction? Each reverberates across the world. Each brings real fortune or failure, happiness or misery, life or death. Some say that long ago the game had its last victory and defeat. That's why this all sits here now, baking in the sun, gathering dust, cracking and wearing away in a fading world."

"You don't believe that, though," said Jade.

Rucksack shook his head. "I fear this game is only on pause. If play continues someday, I fear the fate o' this game will be the fate o' the world too."

"You want me to keep a light heart after that?"

"The key to flying is a light heart. To soar whenever you want means finding a light heart no matter what else you feel," said Rucksack. "I know all the guilt, pain, and hardship this beautiful wretched feckin world can throw at you. The fate o' the world has been on my shoulders more times than you've had a pint, Jade Bluegold. I still found a way to fly."

"Then how did you manage it?"

"I didn't stop feeling the pain and the fear and the horrible vomity squashy feeling in my stomach," said Rucksack. "But I found the love and joy anywhere I could, despite all else. Sometimes, because o' all else."

Jade nodded. "Because otherwise, the despair was all you had."

"It's one thing to feel despair," said Rucksack. "It's quite another to let it be in charge. Love. Joy."

Jade nodded. "No matter what else." It started to make sense.

"You always have to come back to those," said Rucksack. "Find those, and you can fly. Feck, find those, and you can do anything, take on anything, no matter the weight or the task or the fate." He pointed toward the boulder. "Now quit stalling and have another go."

Closing her eyes a moment, Jade sought it out again. The happy memory. The sense of joy. But there weren't many of those for her to find. Childhood had been in short supply of sincere smiles. So had much of adulthood.

But there was one. In her mind, she reached for it.

That moment in the garden. The world frozen. Bird in mid-air. His outstretched arm, the ring glinting in the light.

That was the joy. Not his about-to-be-asked question. But the moment The Management had appeared—the moment they had offered her the choice.

She was different. There was a different fate ahead for her, if only she chose it above all else.

"Of course I said yes," Jade whispered to herself.

She held it. The moment they asked and she answered and her entire life changed.

Eyes closed, she jumped.

Rucksack chuckled. "Not bad, Bluegold. Not bad at all."

Jade opened her eyes. She wasn't flying, wasn't holding steady —but neither was she falling or already eating more dirt. She wobbled, unsteady, still vertical, the ground visible below her black boots. But she stayed up. The joy spread through her, the lightness and exultation. Freed from the earth, untethered in the sky. It might not be flying—but she already knew the elation in her heart. That taste of lightness. And how she wanted to do it again. Like an autumn leaf, Jade fluttered to the ground. She stumbled a little as she landed—but she didn't fall.

As her feet touched the earth, Rucksack came over and clapped her on the shoulder. "Reminds me o' the first time I started to get it," he said. "That's a good start for today. We can build on it more tomorrow."

Jade's eyes widened. "What? Are we stopping now?" She shook her head. "But I'm starting to get it!"

Rucksack shrugged. "All right then. Go for it. I know you won't hear anything different. I certainly didn't."

"Light heart," said Jade. "How could my heart not be any lighter than it is right now?"

She all but leaped to the top of the boulder. With hardly a moment's pause, eyes wide, she leaped off the top.

And ate more Tibetan dirt. At least nothing broke this time.

Rucksack helped her up. "That's why," he said. "Because that first taste o' it is wonderful—but fear and regret aren't the only things that can weigh down the heart. Even excitement can be its own undoing."

Jade spat out dirt. "Why?"

"The weight o' expectation," he said. "You got the concept. You hovered. That first moment, that first taste, is more intoxicating than every variety of booze in every pub in the world. And when you went back up, what were you thinking about?'

"I was thinking about how it felt to fly," said Jade. "I thought that would be enough."

"Quite the opposite. The key to the heart is not to think about the heart. You have to forget all else in this life but that bit o' pure, ultimate, from-the-heart-to-the-heart joy. To fly is to be, no matter what else. Then, and only then, can you fly."

"But you can't do that anymore."

"No." A sad quiet fell flat through Rucksack's voice, and for a moment he turned away. "I haven't yet found that lightness again. If you could hold my heart, you would know that all my mistakes and regrets have made it as heavy as the world. All the guilt from all the pain and suffering caused by The Blast—caused by my failure to prevent it."

"But you keep trying."

Rucksack nodded. "Joy and love above all else," he said. "Even if I never fly again, joy and love are where I'm aiming. If I can, I'll find the peace I need despite my flaws and mistakes. When that happens, my heart will become as light as sunlight." He smiled. "Guilt, regret, sadness, or anger may be part o' us. Yet when we can put that in the right context, we can lighten our hearts. When we can lighten our hearts, we can fly."

They looked north, toward where someday they would find the Heart of the World.

"The Heart's not what people say nowadays," said Rucksack.

"Or at least it wasn't the last time I was there, and that was centuries ago." The sadness had come back to his voice.

"You feel guilty that you haven't visited your grandparents," said Jade. "Everyone feels that."

Her own grandparents had been the only kind, bright spot in her hard dark life. They had looked nothing alike, but Jade could feel that they shared similar hearts. She hadn't seen them since she had left, all those years ago. She had never written either, for fear that she might be found. Her own sadness came over her. Her grandparents knew nothing of Jade.

Wait. That wasn't true.

They knew one thing.

The Management's operative had told Jade's grandparents in person.

The last thing they knew was that their granddaughter was dead.

Jade's eyes were heavy, hot, and stinging. She looked away.

There was no way she could fly right now.

"I feel guilty about many things," said Rucksack, his voice gentle as he came near. "My grandparents taught me so much. Flying, but so much more. Fighting. Negotiation. They taught me to use my body, my mind, and my heart as one. They trained me, so that when the time was right, I could become, well, Faddah feckin Rucksack."

He shook his head. "I'm ashamed for them to see me, when I've added so much to the suffering they find unbearable about the world. They know about The Blast. It might have happened on the other side o' the world, but I fear most o' all the damage it may have done here."

"You're afraid the Heart has changed," said Jade, "has given in to some sort of darkness and sadness."

Rucksack sighed. "It's not impossible. I don't know what's there. I don't know what it's like. When I was last there... Because o' The Blast, sometimes I have a hard time with my memories. I remember a great despair there, the last time I came to the Heart. They had been there so long, sometimes I fear that they were losing hope."

"In people and the world," said Jade. "How long have they been there?"

"Eons," said Rucksack. "They're immortals. Not gods, but a different sort o' person. They embody all the things humans want to be, but instead o' wishing them, the people o' the Heart live them. The Heart o' the World that I knew was a place o' creativity and peace, innovation and plenty. They wanted, some-day, to leave the Heart. My grandparents would tell me that they wanted to bring the Heart o' the World to the rest o' the world. They wanted to help people have more hope and perseverance, wanted to help solve the ills that plague this world."

Rucksack's face darkened. "But I don't know. It's been so long... and with The Blast... it could be because o' The Blast, they decided they could never emerge. They might have given up. The rumors could be truer than I realize. If the Heart has gone dark..." He shook his head. "I can't rule it out."

Jade touched his shoulder and looked him deep in the eyes, taking in all the sadness etched deep into his face. "They might have gone dark and despairing," she said. "They might all be dead. We don't know. We'll only know if we go there. We'll find what we can. And we'll do what we can."

"If they are gone," said Rucksack, "or lost or dead, then it's another thing that's my fault."

"I don't believe that," said Jade. "Even if it weighs on your heart, I won't let it weigh on mine. There's a chance you're wrong. There's a chance the Heart is not dark. Even if you can't believe that, I'll do it for you. I'll keep my heart light, because despite all you fear, their could be light too. We won't know until we get there. But look, teacher, you gotta believe what you're telling me. Even a weary heart can find lightness and joy, and even a little can carry you through darkest hardships."

"I may have to start calling you teacher." Rucksack tried to find a small smile. "That's a great kindness you've done me."

Jade smiled. "It's the least I can do. You're not a totally wretched teacher after all."

They started walking again. Jade stared north. She wondered when they would get their first look at the Heart of the World. The massive mountain would be rising above all others. It was taller than Everest, Rucksack had said. It had stood for eons, but if the enemy was there, it could soon fall.

Jade's own face darkened now. She had no idea what they were walking into. They had no help. They had no strategy, and not enough to go on to make one. Jade tried not to fall into her own despair. She hoped the enemy didn't know they were coming. She sighed. If any love or joy was shining on the other side of that fear, she sure as hell couldn't see it anywhere.

14

———

CLOUD

From the game board of the world, Jade and Rucksack passed through more hills. The rocks were grayer, less round, the beginning of peaks. The brilliant white of pure unsullied snow glinted all around. Gleaming bands of ice striped the surrounding hills and mountains.

As the sun lowered in the sky, the chill on the wind had a bite that Jade hadn't felt until now. Jade and Rucksack's path sloped upward, over another hill, then up another, higher and higher. The thin air burned at Jade's lungs and throat. Her body was adapting, but with a struggle. Jade wondered what the peak of tolerance was for her enhanced body. When would it give out?

Up she and Rucksack trekked, the steep terrain almost vertical now. Small rocks bounced down past them, and Jade forced herself not to look back. Then, of course, she looked back. The barren, pebbly landscape tumbled down far below. It didn't level out until a distance that, if she did fall, she did not believe she could recover from.

Healing wasn't the same thing as immortality or invulnerability. Jade knew she could die. If life were on one side of a line and death on another, she didn't know where the line was.

Creeping up the steep slope, Jade understood for the first time that there was a line. She also understood how thin and tenuous that thread was. So slight a thing was all that prevented her crossing from life to death.

At the top of the hill, Rucksack had them pause. "Let's have a look at where we are," he said. "It's been some time since I was here. We are getting closer to the Heart, but I for one don't exactly want to rush on to get there."

Jade didn't need any persuading. They sat on the bare hilltop and gazed north. "There," said Jade, pointing not north, but a little west. A thin gray plume stretched into the sky, fading into the deepening blue of late afternoon.

Rucksack touched his hand to the earth. Jade nodded. She had felt it too, the rumbling in the earth, the low pain of the splitting world.

"What do you think is attacking the Heart?" said Jade.

"I wish I knew," said Rucksack. His skin had paled. His voice grew distant, as if he had fled to some distant part of the world, some old memory or adventure.

"What are you not telling me?" said Jade. A breeze was blowing from the west, and Jade tucked her hair out of her face.

"Lots," replied Rucksack. "Ten thousand years, Jade. There's a lot I don't say. And won't, unless I decide I should."

"But you've encountered danger after danger. Monster after monster. Demons and gods."

"That's what the stories say." Rucksack shrugged. "I faced what needed facing. I did what needed doing. Stories only tell you what happened from the comfort o' it having already happened. I didn't live those stories. I lived the challenge and the uncertainty, the terror and the danger. Stories make it seem like you're following a set path. But when you are making the choices, trying to find the right thing among a mess o' bad, there is no certainty. Often one mistake was all that stood between the world drawing another breath and the end o' all things."

Far on the horizon, Jade watched a V-shaped cloud moving north. Her eyes narrowed. That didn't make sense. She stared more closely at the cloud, trying to take in every detail. Around it, other clouds moved too. Except they weren't moving north. They were moving east, on the same western breeze that was blowing against her left cheek. Ahead of them, high in the air, the clouds rushed by on the whipping wind.

But even that wasn't what troubled her.

She stood.

"What is it?" said Rucksack.

"That cloud," replied Jade. "It's moving in its own direction. It's not moving like the other clouds are. But that's not all." She couldn't bear to say it.

"It's what?"

"It's the same. The same as a cloud I saw on the train ride, when I thought I was going to Agamuskara. I saw that exact same cloud. And I saw it again, only I didn't think about it as that cloud. Because why would that occur to me? Clouds change. They're not the same. They're never the same. Clouds are always changing."

Rucksack nodded. "That's true."

Jade turned and stared at him. "Except?"

"Except why can't clouds stay the same? We only think they change. But there's no reason they have to."

"But clouds do change. You can lie on a hillside and watch them shift and transform."

She stared north. It was definitely the same massive cloud. It moved a little farther, until it floated above the high, jagged, broken summit of a tall broad mountain. Judging by how nothing surrounded it, the mountain looked like it stood alone in a clear plain. The rest of the mountains ringed it, yet this lonely mountain stood apart from them. Bands of white snow and ice covered the other mountains. But the gray and brown peak was clear.

Above the jagged summit, the cloud stopped moving. Its

narrow, jagged bottom floated in place above the broken mountain. They didn't quite touch, though, and a wide band of blue sky remained visible between them.

The other clouds were ants rushing past an elephant standing still.

"Aye," said Rucksack. "Clouds change." A wistful note crept into his voice, and a small smile broke over his face like sunrise. The fire in his eyes glowed now, stars in the night sky. "Unless they're a cloud fortress."

"A cloud... fortress?"

"That's the funny thing," said Rucksack. "It's exactly what it sounds like. A fortress. Made o' cloud. It's funny how words reflect truth. The old English word for cloud is *clud*, or clod, and it meant a mass o' rock, a hill."

"But clouds... you know, they're water and dust."

"They are. But so is mud when you get right to it. Mud is mud, unless you know how to work it, turn it into clay. All things can be more than we realize. Dust can become brick and mortar. Iron rusts and breaks—unless you know how to forge it into steel."

"You're telling me that you know how to forge a cloud... into a stronghold?"

Rucksack nodded. His eyes shone. "I never thought I'd see it again." His voice was a little jagged. "Ten thousand years, Jade Bluegold. Saving the world. Helping wherever life needed me to be. In all that time, you can't stay in one place. I learned that I needed to have little hidey-holes, you see. Places where I could recharge, or heal, or store supplies."

"So you would go somewhere and make—what?—a little room?"

"When you lived in Hong Kong, do you remember walking by places," said Rucksack. "Say, between two buildings, and you'd see some strange door, set back a little ways? Or you know how so many places have doors that no one ever sees open, and you never see anyone going in or out?"

Jade nodded, though she also tucked away something else in her thoughts for later.

"A lot o' those are mine," said Rucksack. "Little rooms in buildings or off narrow alleys. Doors that make no sense and seem to have no purpose. A few caves. Some basements and attics. The odd house or flat that you swear must be empty. There are bits all over this world where I've got a bed and a few tools or books tucked away, maybe a little eating space. And a few dusty bottles o' stout, o' course. When I need to plan or recover, or tuck away from the world awhile, I'm always near one o' my wee places."

"You must have hundreds."

Rucksack shrugged. "Could be thousands. It's one o' the things I have a hard time remembering. Pretty sure I've walked by some and not recognized them for what they are. But that doesn't happen often. At least, I guess it doesn't. If I've forgotten I suppose I don't rightly know."

Other clouds rushed by it, but the massive cloud stayed still and floated above the mountain. Jade looked at it more closely. The mountain's jagged top made it look like the peak had been ripped off. Or exploded off, she realized, by some massive force from within. But the cloud. She stared and wondered.

"Jade?"

And forgot Rucksack was there.

"Jade?"

"The cloud," she said at last. "It looks just like the mountain. Only upside down."

"Inverted, actually," said Rucksack.

"They completely mirror one another. It's like looking at the reflection of a mountain in the water," said Jade. "Only instead of seeing the bases touch, mountain and reflection, it's the summits. I don't understand. This can't be possible."

"O' course it's possible, you eejit," said Rucksack. 'Learning the truth doesn't change the world. It changes your understanding o' the world. If it's happening, it's more than possible. It's actual."

From top to bottom, the cloud exactly mirrored the dimensions and angles of the mountain. Jade couldn't make out the broad top of the cloud, though. Wisps and bands of gray, silvery cloud, thicker than the rest, covered it, concealing it from view.

"Oh my goddess," said Jade Bluegold. The wonder hit her now, washing through her, widening her eyes and dropping her jaw open. "It's... It's beautiful. It's magnificent. And you built this... from cloud." She stared again at the mountain.

"That's the Heart of the World," she said.

"Aye," replied Rucksack. "Though seeing it and getting to it are different things."

A glow went through Jade. All the hard days, all the dust, all the falls and injuries, all the wandering in the middle of nowhere. Now, at last, she could see it. A glimpse of where she needed to go. Or, at least, the halfway point. Jade tried to calm her pounding heart. Getting there, facing the enemy, saving the world, even those things were only half the journey. There was still the getting back.

"My cloud fortresses have saved my skin hundreds o' times," said Rucksack. "While my hidey-holes have been useful, I realized that I couldn't always be near one. I needed something that could move with me. What better than clouds?"

"I see," said Jade. "They're always there, passing through—like you. No one pays attention to them—like you. And clouds change. They move. They pass, out of sight and out of mind."

"And they are indistinct," said Rucksack. "No one would ever think twice about a cloud being anything other than dust and water. Plus, no weapon can harm them, because they're clouds. Yet they come with their own weapons: rain, hail, sleet, lightning. Best part? No one can get close to one—unless they know how to fly." Rucksack shook his head. "A brilliant security system, if I do say so myself."

Jade nodded. "Unless you forget how to fly."

"Aye," said Rucksack. "Not exactly a problem I expected to have."

"That's why you want to learn again," said Jade. "You saw one of your cloud fortresses and remembered what it was."

Rucksack nodded. "It was this one that reminded me, actually," he said. "Months ago. I'd completely forgotten about my cloud fortresses. Then I saw this one pass overhead. O' all the fortresses I built, none equaled this one. It's the biggest, the most complex."

"A masterpiece," said Jade. "In cloud."

"That's all I remember o' why I made it, though," he said. The small sadness returned to his voice. "I wanted to see how far I could take it, how big, how well I could shape the cloud."

"Was it going north then too?"

"It was. At the time I wondered what that could mean. If it kept its course, it made me wonder if it might be going to the Heart. The fortresses have a way of going where they're needed, even if it's not where you intended to go at the time."

"You crafted it to match the actual Heart." Jade stared at the mountain and the cloud again. "And we're getting close."

"Another couple o' days trekking," said Rucksack. "When you turned up and the cloud had passed, I was certain something was wrong at the Heart. The two call to each other."

"You built this thousands of years ago, but this has never happened before, has it—the fortress going to the Heart?"

Rucksack shook his head. "They never needed to. What few people knew o' the Heart, the knowledge either died with them, or it passed into legend." He looked at her, a sincerity passing over his face like cloud. "I'm glad you found me, Jade. I'm glad we're facing this together."

"Same here," replied Jade. She stared at the cloud fortress. "Is there anything inside we can use to help us?"

"There might be." Rucksack shrugged and looked away, his head tilting down. His dark eyes blushed with embarrassment. "But I can't remember."

"We'll figure it out," said Jade. "We don't have a lot of daylight left, though. We'd better make our way down and set camp for the night."

Even as the cloud fortress and the Heart of the World left her sight, they stayed with Jade's mind and heart. But so did a nagging question. "I have to ask," said Jade, her voice trailing off.

"Oh, the toilets were the easiest part," said Rucksack. "When you're floating up so high, everything pretty much dissipates into the wind."

Something else occurred to her. "There are all these reports over the centuries," said Jade. "Strange storms that rain weird things onto the ground, like frogs, meat, fish, worms, even money. I don't suppose you had anything to with those?"

Rucksack chuckled. "I might've done." He winked. "Just because I'm always saving the world, doesn't mean I can't have fun with it now and again too."

15

———

GAP

So close now.

All through the prior day they had raced over the barren landscape. The thin air cut. The hills and mountains no longer blocked the wind. Now they channeled it. Sometimes the gusts punched strongly enough to knock Jade and Rucksack off their feet.

They emerged from a narrow pass and paused. Jade caught a small glimpse again of the cloud fortress, and a little of the mountaintop below. Worn beige fields of rubble surrounded them. The two of them continued their slow way down through the winding mountains.

"We have to get through one more stretch of mountains," said Rucksack. "The Heart o' the World stands in the midst o' an otherwise empty plain, but a ring o' mountains surrounds it."

"Once we're there," said Jade, "we'll have to be more careful than ever. We still don't know what we'll be facing, and we'll be exposed."

Rucksack nodded. "Our best guess is that the attack is happening at the west o' the mountain. I'll take us on a route that should give us the advantage o' being able to assess while staying out o' sight."

"We'll know soon enough." Jade's voice was cold and grim as the wind shoved her. The trekking was hard over the rough ground. At least the exertion helped her think less about how cold she was. The roars and whistles of the gusts seemed to get their kicks out of reminding her.

"Why do you think The Management chose me?" she asked.

"Because you were kind to a thief," said Rucksack. "So they said."

"Yes, that's what they said," replied Jade. "But The Management are like you. They never tell the whole story. They told me the truth, but I keep thinking that it wasn't a complete truth. They left something out. Something they didn't want me to know."

"I can't say I know," said Rucksack. "The Management hasn't exactly made my acquaintance." Before them, a sheer vertical brown wall rose hundreds of feet in the air. The face was blank, featureless, except for one thing. Rucksack nodded toward a tall, narrow gap in the rocks ahead, as if some goddess had sliced through the mountain from top to base.

"One more bit," said Rucksack, "but I'm afraid this is nothing compared to what's ahead." He paused. "See you on the other side," he said. "I hope."

Before Jade could say anything, he passed through the tight gap. His broad body scraped against the rock, and the sound made Jade wince. As he disappeared from sight, Jade shook her head. She thought about what Rucksack had said about her living in Hong Kong, the day he had explained his hidey-holes. The Management weren't the only ones not saying all they knew.

She had to confront him. But the time wasn't right. Yet.

She wouldn't say all she knew either. For now. She didn't like what he had said as he entered the gap, though. Jade stood outside, touching the rock, staring through the gap. It was a slice in the rock. Why did he seem uncertain about her following?

She shook her head, pushing away the doubts crowding her resolve. The sooner through, the sooner they could continue. She took a step inside.

Though Jade was less broad than Rucksack, it was as if the gap shrank. Where there had been space, now was only rock, and it squeezed her so hard it was difficult to breathe.

Jade turned sideways, so she was looking over her left shoulder. The rock pressed against the front and back of her body. The wind rushed at its worst here, an invisible knife stabbing into her right side. Needles of compressed gusts screamed into her ears. She risked turning her head to look back toward the way they had come. The wind slapped at her eyes, the dust and grit almost blinding her.

As soon as Jade was inside, the gap went dark. She could no longer see the way they had come.

The brown rock faded into a deep black, as if a door had shut behind her, trapping her not in a gap between rocks, but in a cave. Jade looked up. Darkness was her roof—sunless, starless, lightless. Looking ahead, all was dark. No Rucksack. No end of the gap. No world beyond. Only darkness. It was as if she had gone into a cave, and the hungry void had swallowed her.

The darkness sank into Jade too, and she stopped moving forward. From the outside, the gap had seemed so short. But inside, she must have walked for miles. For hours. Days. There was no way out. The enemy had laid some sort of trap for them. Or Rucksack had betrayed her. Had he realized what she knew, what she suspected? There was no light to come again. There was only the darkness and the freezing chill, until the moment when even those would become no more. Sooner or later the exposure would overwhelm even her Jade healing, and she would die.

A tear fell and froze on her face. Jade's breath hitched as she tried to breathe, but the gap was even tighter now. Even her lungs couldn't move. No, it wouldn't be exposure that killed her. The mountain was the trap. It was crushing her with every trudge forward. Every attempt to breathe was met with another tightening of the mountain's death squeeze. Would she asphyxiate first? Or would the mountain crush her flat and red? She wondered how long the red would stain the brown. Or if it would all soak in quickly and be gone, leaving no sign of the mountain's satisfied hunger.

Jade's eyes narrowed. "No," she said.

She wasn't dying here. She wasn't staying trapped. She hadn't come through all she'd endured to be the filling in a mountain sandwich.

Her eyes narrowed. She yelled, forcing all the air out of her lungs. She scraped past the rocks, pressing her body through, no matter how red and raw the jagged stones cut her.

A jutting bit of rock caught her chest and stopped her. With a growl, then another yell, Jade pushed with all her might. As if the rock were surrendering, the pressure gave way. She shot forward again, so fast she would have stumbled had it not been for the rocks holding her up.

Ahead, at the end of the world, a small dot, a little gleam in the dark, began to shine. At the edge of the brown and black, it shimmered silver and gold.

Jade moved toward the brightening gleam. It pulsed a little, flaring bigger and then smaller. Jade smiled when she understood —it pulsed in time with her beating heart.

Where there was a heart, there was life.

The wind fell away, as if it could no longer blow through the gap. Ahead, so close now, the darkness gave way. The glint stopped pulsing and shone. The little light glowed soft and hazy, but it was there, and steady, and with her every step it grew brighter. The light showed the edges of the narrow gap. From the far edges of the blackness, brown rock emerged. And from the edges of the brown rock, a world glowed beyond.

Jade emerged from the gap. Panting and doubled over, she took in the thin air as if it were the thick stuff of sea level. Even the chill she embraced, as if it were tropical sun. Ahead of Jade, the brown flat rock ended at a sheer cliff edge. A large chasm separated her from the rock beyond, the way through the mountains to get to the Heart.

On a small round boulder, Rucksack sat facing the gap. He stared at Jade, and a look of relief and joy lit up his face.

"You could have told me," said Jade.

He shook his head. "It's different for everyone,' he said. "Some things can't be warned about. They can only be gotten into. And, hopefully, gotten through."

"Why?"

He shrugged. "Sometimes I think the world wants to see what we do when we see the worst o' the world and o' ourselves," he said. "The world wants to see what we're made o'."

"That's why you said you hoped to see me on the other side," she said. "I'd be in the heart of something terrible, and I'd have to find something better in myself to pull me through."

"I believed you could do it," said Rucksack. "Otherwise we never would have made it this far."

"But in this world, you don't know something's true until it actually happens," replied Jade.

Rucksack nodded. Jade told him of the pressure, the darkness, the despair. When she finished she asked, "What was it like for you?"

A tear, like her own, had frozen to Rucksack's cheek. "Fire," he said, and his voice trembled. "Like a star exploding in the sky, but right above you and all around you. I wasn't closed in like you were. I was on a hill, walking and walking. Then I was on a black road, surrounded by ash, but also surrounded by fire. The fire was everywhere, Jade. Surrounding me. Overhead. A mile-wide rope o' it, a field o' fire burning all the world and leaving its scar." As he spoke, he clenched and unclenched his gloved left hand, as if it pained him.

"I've never known darkness like that," said Jade.

"I've known that fire, though." Rucksack's sad voice was far away. "That's exactly what it was like in The Blast."

"How did you get through?"

"Then or now?"

Jade shrugged. "Both."

"Same way you did a moment ago," said Rucksack. "I decided what I would say yes to, what I would say no to, and I kept moving forward."

Jade sat down next to him and touched his shoulder. They said nothing. They breathed. They tried to remind themselves that they had come through. They had both survived. They had made it—and they could continue.

Then, in the windless silence, the world shook. The not-so-far-off attack intensified, and the Heart of the World screamed its suffering. It was as if the very rock itself was yelling in fear, terror, and agony.

Jade leaped up. "We've got to get there, Rucksack. Before it's too late."

"Yes, but—"

Jade ran to the cliff edge. She stopped, barely, before careening over.

A thousand feet below, a river foamed as it raced through jagged rocks sticking out of the water. Hundreds of yards away, the other cliff face stood.

No bridge ran between them.

STEP

Rucksack pulled her back.

"It's as bad as you think," he said. "There's no bridge. The sheer cliff is impossible to climb—and even if you did attempt it, it's so perilous that any fall would be your death. It might even kill me, something I'm in no hurry to test."

"Even if we did climb down, we'd be too weary to go on," said Jade. "Yet we'd still have to cross the river—which is much wider than it looks. And we'd still have to climb up the other side." She shook her head. "There is no way across. Did you know about this?"

"O' course," he replied. "I've been here before, remember? The Heart isn't a place you simply stroll into."

"It's a quest," said Jade. "I get it. We're being tested to see if we deserve to get to the Heart. Can't they let you go up to the door and knock, and tell you to bugger off if they don't think you should be able to come in?"

"They saw all the goodness and horror o' the world, Jade," replied Rucksack. "If you and I knew what they've known, we may also tuck ourselves into a mountain and rip up the welcome mat."

"What did they see?"

"Thousands upon thousands o' years ago, before my parents' time, the people o' the Heart saw a world willing to harm. They saw a people obsessed with tossing love aside for the sake o' gaining and using power. They tried to counter it." Rucksack shook his head. "Threadbare love has always struggled to combat power's allure. It had come to a horrible decision: war or retreat. The people o' the Heart decided that they could not bear combat. They couldn't swallow the supposed ideal that it would be for the greater good. You know, being willing to kill someone now because their blood makes things shiny later. Instead o' violence, the people o' the Heart left. One day they were all around the world. The next they were gone. They came here, and have been in the mountain ever since. My grandparents told me they will return to the world only when the world is ready to choose love over power again."

"We have a ways to go," said Jade, not hiding the bitterness in her voice.

"Aye," said Rucksack. "But I suspect that's another reason The Management chose you."

"I'm no poster child of love. I chose being a Jade over love, in fact."

"Did you do it for power?"

Jade shook her head. "I did it because I wanted to help. I understood that throughout my life, what I've wanted to do, all I've wanted to do, was help. I had never known that, until the moment The Management appeared to me."

"Perhaps The Management want to send the people o' the Heart a sign that the time for them to return is coming. So they sent you."

Rucksack smiled and walked to the edge of the cliff. "Keep all that in mind right now," he said. "There is no bridge here. But there is a way across. Remember: The way to the Heart o' the World never has anything to do with the work o' the mind. To get to the Heart, you must use your own heart. To use your heart is to trust, to have faith, to take a chance. That's why it's said that you can only get to the Heart if you do not know the way. You have to forget that you are going there. Once you stop thinking about it, you can let your truest self get on with getting there."

He smiled. "Let's go to the other side, Jade Bluegold."

"I take it you're about to leave me on my own again," said Jade.

Rucksack grinned and shook his head. "Not this time." He held out his bare right hand.

Jade's left hand shook as she took his hand. "What do we do?"

Rucksack grinned. "You already know," he replied. "It's what we do for all these journeys. We take another step."

Before Jade could breathe or prepare herself or anything, they stepped off the edge.

And plummeted toward the rocks and river below.

"Rucksack!" she yelled. "Rucksack!"

"Believe!" he yelled, holding and squeezing her hand. "Trust the world—and trust yourself!"

But fear was everywhere. The fears from where she had grown up. The loneliness in a hard world. The moment when the sun glinted on his ring, that day when she chose and was chosen. Did she choose for love? Or did she choose for power?

The world rushed by.

So much left, never to be returned to. Yet with every decision that had mattered to her, Jade saw inside herself. She did not lead with only her mind. She led with her heart. And she did so now. The Heart of the World awaited—and so did the world's destiny.

Jade opened her eyes. And stumbled forward a step as her feet hit something solid.

"Aye," said Rucksack. His voice shook, but Jade could hear the exhilaration too, and could feel it in his trembling hand. He had stumbled too, but they steadied one another and stood up straight.

Rucksack shook his head. "That feckin first step never gets any easier."

About a hundred feet above them, the brown edge of the cliff sliced into the pale blue sky. Below their feet, they stood on clear air. If Jade squinted and looked down at just the right angle, under her boots she could see a shimmery waviness. A translucent ribbon stretched between the two cliffs.

Step by step, hand in hand, Rucksack and Jade made their way across. Whatever was below them, surrounded them too. It created a tunnel that shielded them from the fierce winds cutting through the canyon.

Jade's heart pounded as she walked over the space below. "This is amazing!"

Rucksack grinned. "Not terrifying?"

Jade shrugged. "Come on, it's a little scary. But when you think you're about to die, and then you don't, for a while everything is amazing again."

Rucksack's laugh boomed around the translucent tunnel. "My grandmother is going to like you a lot, Jade Bluegold."

As they neared the other side, the ribbon sloped upward. Before she knew it, they stepped onto the other side of the cliff. Jade looked back across the chasm, but she could see only the empty air. She turned again and faced the ring of mountains that separated them from the Heart of the World. The scream of the attack surrounded them again. After passing through the gap and crossing the chasm, Jade didn't mind the horrible sound anymore.

"Any more tests and challenges?" said Jade.

"None on the schedule," replied Rucksack. "But I don't know all things."

Jade nodded. "You know you've got to keep going."

Beyond the pass before them, the cloud fortress still floated above its mountain twin. She started forward, Rucksack a step behind, and the Heart of the World, at last, just beyond.

17

FLY

Jade and Rucksack emerged from the ring of mountains to find a world that had fallen silent. Gray and brown mountains ringed a vast empty plain. At the center, the Heart of the World rose. And rose. If the Himalayas were the roof of the world, then the Heart was the pillar holding it all up.

"I didn't know a mountain could be that big," said Jade. "It's bigger than Everest, isn't it?"

"Aye, Chomolungma is far smaller," said Rucksack. "The Heart is taller and broader than any other mountain."

Above the Heart of the World, the cloud fortress floated. The world was still, silent, and serene. Jade leaned back against a rock, feeling weary yet excited.

"It's beautiful here," said Jade. "Desolate. Barren. But there's a purity to it. A reminder that even where there is little or no life, there is still beauty."

"There's few as would say that," said Rucksack. "Especially after all you've been through to get here—and it's not as if you came all o' your own accord."

"All this time, all these hardships," said Jade. "So much uncertainty. Yet we're here."

Rucksack nodded, but his voice was grim. "Now the real work begins."

Jade looked from him to the quiet plain. Whatever was happening at the Heart, maybe the enemy was taking a break.

"You're right." The odd quiet of her voice made Rucksack stare at her.

"Everything okay?"

"O' course," Jade replied, throwing Rucksack's accent back at him. "I need to know something first."

"What could be so important?"

"When you were telling me about your hidey-holes and the cloud fortresses," said Jade. "How did you know I used to live in Hong Kong?"

Rucksack shrugged. "We've been trekking for days, Jade. We've discussed many things. You must've told me."

She shook her head. "I never told you that. I never told you much of anything about my life before becoming a Jade. You knew I was in Hong Kong, though. How?"

"Jade, look—"

"We're about to face goddess knows what," said Jade. "We have no idea what is around or inside that mountain. There could be an army covering the plain. There could be some sort of rogue god who has a score to settle with you and your family. You don't know any more than I do. And right now, I know that you are hiding something from me. I want to trust you. I need to be able to trust you. But I need to know. I've never met you before this little fellowship of the Heart. What do you know about me?"

Rucksack turned away from her, but Jade could see the conflict in his cinched face. Finally, he looked her in the eye. "I was there," he began. "The day The Management appeared to you and asked. I was up on the top floor o' the Tiger Pagoda. I saw everything."

"You saw Declan propose to me," said Jade. "And you saw The Management appear." She paused, brow scrunched. "But the world... The Management pulled me out of time, they said. No one could see."

"As you've pointed out," said Rucksack, "I'm their ghost. They can't control me or influence me, at least not as far as either of us can tell. I see things as they are, Jade Bluegold. The Management can't pull their tricks without me seeing through them."

"Do you know what became of Declan?"

For long, long moments, Rucksack said nothing. 'I do," he said. "But—"

The world ripped apart. It must have. That or a million banshees had been abducted from Ireland to Tibet so they could shriek. The world was exploding from inside out. That had to be it.

Jade and Rucksack both fell to their knees, clutching their ears and closing their eyes. After long, horrible minutes, the sound faded. Jade and Rucksack dared to stand and open their eyes again. They waited a little longer before uncovering their ears. Smoke rose from the western side of the mountain. Large, brilliant flashes of light filled the air, forcing them to look away or risk blindness.

"We've got to move," said Rucksack. "This has to stop."

Jade stared at him, and at the smoke and flashes. She wanted to know. Had to know.

She sighed. But not now. Now she had to do what she had chosen and had been chosen to do.

They ran down the slope, out onto the open plain. They understood, but left unsaid, that the odds were against anyone expecting them. Whatever was blasting the mountain, they wouldn't think anyone would come here. All their attention would be on wielding their vast power.

"I would have thought they'd attack the gate in the eastern side o' the mountain," said Rucksack. "That's as much o' a front door as the Heart gets, so why not try to kick it down? Yet whoever this is, they're not doing that."

"They might not know about the gate," said Jade. Rucksack shrugged. "Or they want to blast their way in because it helps them in some other way."

They arced across the plain toward the mountain. Jade hoped the flashes were hiding their movements.

Rucksack glanced at her. "What did The Management tell you to do?"

"Stop whatever is attacking the Heart," said Jade. "They're not exactly into details, and I don't think they had many. We now know more than they do about whatever the hell is going on here."

"What do you think you're going to do?"

Jade started to reply, but thought a little more first. "I don't know," she said. "This isn't a thinking problem. Whatever is happening at the Heart, it's a problem of the heart. So I'll use mine to deal with it."

They came to an outcropping of rock, the closest they had come now to seeing the force attacking the Heart. Cautiously, slowly, they peered over the rock.

"I don't see an army," said Jade. "Do you?"

"No." Rucksack's voice was flat and cold. While his eyes burned, there was also a wisp of uncertainty in his gaze. "They could be camping in the mountain ring."

"Or it's one being," said Jade. "One force, powerful beyond imagination. They must be close to breaking in."

"Best to assume so," said Rucksack. "But there's no way we can get closer. We go beyond this, they'll see us."

Jade nodded. And looked up the mountain. "Then there's only one thing to do," she said.

"What?"

She pointed up. "We need to fly."

"You're a feckin loony."

She shook her head. "We fly, we gain high ground. We can look down and see what's going on, know the true scope and scale of what we're up against. Plus, no one will expect an attack from above." Jade shrugged. "But if you have a better idea, I'm listening."

Rucksack sighed. "Dammit."

Jade smiled and held out her hand. "Go ahead. Lighten your heart. I'll lighten mine. We'll do this together."

Rucksack took her hand. They stared upward, at a shelf of rock that would hide them yet give them a vantage point. Jade thought of all they had been through. Then she smiled, and she and Rucksack squeezed each other's hands.

Their feet left the earth, and they rose up over the base of the mountain. Jade was certain she heard Rucksack giggle, but it was hard to tell over her own giggling.

The floating from before was nothing compared to this. The world's weight dropped away, and the lightness of Jade's soul blazed through her, beyond her. She could feel the lightness in the air, in the sunshine, even in the rocky slope a few feet from her body as she flew by it. To fly was to taste all that could be. When you flew, you stopped being just a person and became all possibility too.

Slowly they neared the rock shelf. Jade and Rucksack looked down.

"No," said Jade.

"No," said Rucksack.

The weight slammed back into their hearts, and they both began to fall.

18

ADVANTAGE

The mountain scraped and bumped her. Jade tucked her head down. She tried to turn with the careening tumbles and falls to protect her body as best she could. The world bounced and spun. Every time she thought she had reached the bottom of the mountain, she bumped more—or crashed off a nasty rock. Only pain was more constant than the falling and bashing. Her body was trying to keep up with her injuries, but soon hurt would outpace healing.

Then, after the fall, came the stop at the end. Jade slammed the floor of the plain hard with her stomach, knocking the wind out of her. Coughing, she focused, trying to get her body to recover in moments what would take weeks, or even months, for an ordinary person. Nothing seemed broken, thank goodness. Jade clawed into the hard, packed earth, and forced the breath back into her body. They had fallen. They had lost the element of surprise. And the enemy was here.

Oh, goddess, the enemy was here. So much worse than she ever would have let herself imagine.

Jade sensed Rucksack next to her, a puddle of black on the brown earth. Her mind flashed back to when they had met. The horrible fall. The crunch that had been like a rock crashing through her soul. But Rucksack was rising too. Together they leaped from the earth and stood on their feet again.

Stunned by their surprise appearance, the being before them stopped attacking the mountain. Mouth hanging open, the being dropped its hands open and now they lay still. Smoke wafted from them, a remnant of the massive forces that flowed from them like water off a cliff.

Jade had no plan. No strategy. No chance to figure out strengths and weaknesses. Only this one moment.

She leaped forward. Rucksack came around to the left, so that the being would have to fend them off from different angles. Jade put the rest out of her head. Who it was did not matter. Only their actions mattered—and their actions had to be stopped.

Aiming for the head, she punched hard, hoping for a knock-out. From the being's right, Rucksack landed a solid punch in the kidneys.

The being staggered backward, roared, then doubled over. Jade's knee whacked the being in the face. Rucksack followed with a kick to the back of the knees, knocking the being to the ground in a kneeling position. Jade's elbow crunched into the back of the being's head.

It was going to be easier than she had feared, Jade began to realize. The Management had been right to send her, right to set her on this path that had led her to Rucksack, that had led her here. She was only a rookie Jade, plucked from her first assignment to save the world. The glory filled Jade's mind and heart. She would be the greatest of all the Jakes and Jades, beloved by the world and The Management. A hero. She'd be discussed and sung about in legends like Rucksack was. After this, anything would be possible. The past did not matter. Only the present did, and the future that you wanted.

The being sat on its knees, upright but swaying, head rolling, chin rubbing chest.

Save the Heart, save the world. It was time to end this.

Setting her stance wide, one foot behind her, Jade's right fist whistled through the air. A heat blazed in her hand, every ounce of energy and power pouring through this one final punch. Jade wondered what the fist must look like. Did flames trail behind?

She had no idea where the yell came from. And refused to hear what she screamed. The act of the scream was all that mattered—the focusing, the intimidating, the sheer release of power. What she said happened to be what she said. A heat of the moment. Nothing more.

But the word was heard, and the being's head snapped up. A thin stream of blood trickled out of its right nostril. Its eyes, glazed and foggy before, now came into sharp focus. A darkness laughed there, in eyes that had been so blue. And so lovely.

Jade tried to ignore the worst part. The threads of destiny and decision, which wove from all things, did not flow from this being. Those tendrils had been severed, and the creature had been removed from the normal course of existence. It lived apart now. She wondered what that craving must feel like. A distant part of her mind reminded her that Rucksack was the same. Jade wondered what could have happened to cause the being to become so separate from all things. Why had it chosen this path? It could have done so many other things instead. None of them involved trying to break into a mythical mountain and destroy all life in the world.

It stared at her now. The world had slowed, and Jade could see every hair on his head, blond and smooth. No dust covered his handsome face. The roof of the world brought them closer to the sun here, but the being's skin had no tan and was as pale as it had ever been. It was so hard to see someone she knew, someone so beautiful doing something so terrible.

At last. Jade's fist was there, in the final centimeters before she could knock him out and end this.

The man's hand shot up and closed around Jade's fist.

At the contact, his eyes blazed up, the blue flaring amidst golden and black. His eyes brimmed with power and intelligence like an overfilled pint. Something else glinted there, dark and hard and sharp, but Jade couldn't tell what. He squeezed her hand. Her knuckles rasped against his palm. So close to his face. So close to it all being over.

But not enough.

The man's mouth arced into a thin smile. "My turn." His dry voice rasped with a deep emotion that Jade could not yet name. Her own surprise was still too sharp. It extinguished the fire of her power, and she did not know what to do next.

Rucksack lunged forward now. The man's eyes twitched to the right. His hand did too, turning so that Jade's bending wrist forced her to follow. The man flung her into Rucksack's path. He stumbled over her, and both Jade and Rucksack smacked the ground hard again.

The man stood up before they did. The blood ran back up his nose. He angled and turned his neck so that loud cracks echoed around them.

Jade scrambled up onto her hands and feet. But the man raised a hand, and she could not move anymore. The force coming at her lowered Jade's body back to the ground. She found herself kneeling, hands behind her, wanting to rise but unable. Next to her, Rucksack was on his knees too, as trapped and stilled as she was.

"Faddah Rucksack," said the man. The disgust in his voice was its own power. Though the man stayed where he was, Rucksack's head swung to one side, as if he had been backhanded. A red mark flashed onto the left side of his face.

The man said nothing for a moment. He stood there, looking at Jade. Surprised? Hopeful? Amazed? Confused? Jade couldn't tell. There was no listening to him, no understanding anything about his body, mind, or heart. Maybe there never had been.

"Jade?" said the man at last. His voice was the only place

where she could tell anything. And everything she had speculated, she found there: surprise, confusion, anger, even joy. But above all, she figured out the emotion she hadn't been able to identify before. After the shock of recognition, Jade found a lingering, struggling hope.

"Jade?" he said again. With that one word the hope shot up in him again, like a drowning swimmer surging out of the water and gasping for life.

Jade nodded. "It's me." Her voice was tight and quiet, and tears strained at her eyes. "But I never thought I'd see you here, Declan."

19

FURY

For a little while, the pain stopped. Jade's cuts healed. So did Rucksack's. Every time they did, Declan raised his smoking hands to his face and laughed.

Laughed.

In the frigid, silent darkness at the far edge of night, Jade and Rucksack kneeled on stiff knees. No light had shone, as if somehow the starlight and moonlight knew they were not welcome. Or they were too scared to shine on Declan.

The night had been long and full of pain, but the tears hurt worst of all. They came down Jade's face, and she could not wipe them away. Jade looked at Declan now, trying to find the man she had known. The man she had loved. Or thought she had loved. Had this been his true self all along?

Instead of resuming the torture, Declan lowered his hands. He looked at Jade but nodded toward Rucksack. "Has he told you the truth?"

"What truth?"

"About why I'm here." Declan ran the fingers of one hand up his other hand, all the way up his arm, then up the side of his face to the top of his head. "About why I'm the way I am." His fingers waggled his hair. "See?" he said. "No more strings on me."

The color left Jade's face. Not only did he know about the helixes; he knew that his own were gone. "How do you know about that?" she asked.

"How fascinating that you know. I've learned so much, Jade, since the day you left me in Hong Kong." His voice had arced higher and higher in pitch, but now it crashed to the ground, low with a fury like a growl. "Since the day you chose to leave me."

"No," said Jade.

"I wasn't supposed to know," said Declan, and the rage crackled in his voice. "I know. It was all supposed to be wiped from my mind and heart. I was supposed to receive tragic news that you had died. It's an excellent cover story."

If he knew the truth... Jade's eyes widened. Who else now knew?

Declan leaned down and pinned Jade's gaze with the hot needle of his own. "Don't worry. I haven't told anyone." He sneered and straightened. "Yet."

Jade lowered her head and closed her eyes, lost in the currents of disgust and relief flooding her.

"I didn't know," she said at last. "I didn't know what had happened to you."

"Because no one would tell you," said Declan, "or because you loved your new life so much that you couldn't be bothered to ask?"

He had not touched her, but the words still slapped and stung.

"But we were talking about Rucksack," said Declan, and he looked away from her and back toward Rucksack. Jade found she could move a little. She couldn't get off the ground or kick Declan in the head, but at least she could blink again. "Rucksack never told you the truth," continued Declan. "Or at least not the whole truth."

Rucksack wouldn't meet her eye.

"You didn't just see what happened in the Gardens," said Jade. "You saw what happened to Declan."

"Oh no. No no no," said Declan, his voice rising to a high whine. "He didn't only watch. He helped make me."

"Hong Kong," said Jade, eyes wide. "No. The Hong Kong Incident... What happened to Jake Hongkong... All those people who had to forget... That was all you?"

The blood had seeped into the floor and could not be cleaned out, she'd heard. The Management had closed the pub where it had happened. They opened a different location, rather than have another Jake or Jade endure day after day where the Hong Kong Incident had happened.

"You know so much," said Declan. "More than I would have expected. Like your being here." He squatted down and looked at her, face close to her own, but she turned away. "You've been up to so much these past few years, my dear Jade," he said. "How I hope you'll choose to tell me what."

Jade tried to ignore Declan's voice. His hot breath fumed dry and sour, like a sick person with a high fever.

"Rucksack," she said. "Tell me the truth now."

"I was at the pub, Jade," he said. "I wanted to stop Declan from losing his destiny, but I couldn't."

"I lost my future, my past, my present, my everything, because of you," said Declan. "And from that loss, I became a killer. Thanks to you. One moment my life was one thing, and the next it was something else. I could remember Jade being in front of me. I was on one knee, holding out the box, finally brave enough to ask. I remember it glinting in the sun, and it was so bright and beautiful. Then it was as if I breathed in and stood at the brink of the world becoming all I could ever hope to become. Then I breathed out, and all was different. The memories started to fade so quickly, Jade, so quickly. They were draining from me like water from an unplugged sink. I could see you fading in my mind, that last sight of you standing before me. It was leaving me, Jade, like you did. Not even the memory would stay."

Jade's eyes burned at the pain she had caused him. "I never meant to hurt you," she said.

"Our intentions don't matter," said Declan. "Only our actions." He stood and nodded toward Rucksack. "Then, as it was all disappearing, this little rock falls in front of me and clatters on the ground."

As if in pain, Rucksack closed his eyes.

"I picked up the rock, and suddenly I could hold everything else in my memory again. My Jade wasn't dead, but she wasn't there with me anymore either. I understood, I think, more quickly than I realized at the time. You already knew what I was going to ask. Whatever happened, whatever you did next, you chose something other than me."

Jade had nothing to say. She could see it now. The feeling she had not been able to name before. Behind the fury, intertwined with all Declan's words, actions, and breath.

Fury didn't burn alone there. Pain blazed there too. Agony. His every movement and moment was his own torment.

"I went to the pub. I confronted the one I thought responsible, but I didn't see you, Rucksack. Cowering in the crowd, were you? I hear stories, you know, that you're some hero, some great legend." Declan shook his head. "You're a coward. You can't even save yourself now."

Declan punched him hard in the face. Rucksack fell over and did not get up. Declan stared at Jade. "I lost my destiny that day," said Declan. "Because of the three of you. Jake Hongkong, at least I've dealt with him. I lost my destiny in the bargain, but maybe that price wasn't as bad as I originally thought. Rucksack caused the circumstances. But you. Oh my Jade." Declan leaned in close to her again. "You are the reason I suffer. You are my agony. My every day, torture and torment. Because of you."

Then he smiled, and it was still a beautiful smile. Not a smile of madness or a chaotic mind. It was an elegant smile, a smile that could have lit the world. But now it showed the darkness behind the beauty.

"My actions torture me," said Declan. A hollow, horrible, quiet loneliness crept into his voice. "I have not wanted to do the things I have done, but I have done them. Whatever you have been doing all these past years, I have been doing much too. Learning much. Now, finally, I understand. I know the nature of the world. I know why my life is the way it is. I know why I do not have happiness, or destiny, or hope, or any sense of possibility."

For a moment, Jade squeezed her eyes shut. She could sense the pain he lived. She could see in her mind the long years he had spent, causing suffering because of his own suffering.

"It doesn't have to be this way," said Jade.

"It doesn't," Declan agreed. "But it is. Our world is the sum of the choices we make. And the world is torture and torment. Nothing more." Declan smiled again. "I understand now, though. I see the answer. It's so simple, like the most elegant answers are." He looked from her to the mountain, and he smiled. Then he looked back at Jade. "I want it all to end. Life, the world, everything. The only way to end the suffering is to end existence."

"That is... That is wrong. Life is more than suffering," said Jade. "Life is love and laughter, friendship and striving. Life is choosing to do what you can with what happens to you."

"True!" said Declan. "I'm so glad we agree. So many times, Jade, so many dark days and nights, I have considered ending my life. Bowing out of this horror. But I don't know what comes next. What if I come back and can do nothing? In this life, such as it is, I can do something about the problem of suffering. I finally understand my life's work and purpose. By staying alive I will bring the world to its end, which will also bring the world to the end of its suffering. It is the only kindness I have, Jade, but it is also the only one that matters."

Jade leaned back, unable to move much, but terrified of him. Released, his festering fury would burn down the world.

"The key to it, as you somehow know, is inside that mountain," said Declan. "I break in there, to this sad little Heart of the World place, then the end of the world begins with the end of the Heart."

"Then why are you bothering with us?" said Jade. "Why not kill us and be done? You want to destroy all things, why distract yourself?"

Declan turned back to face her. His smile curled so high she wondered if the corners of his lips would smack into his eyes. "I admit, you are a surprise, but a pleasant one. Sometimes we must change grand plans in little moments," he said. "I want revenge first. I want to kill Rucksack—after he's suffered enough, that is. He will die no matter what."

Declan squatted down again, his face centimeters from Jade's. "But I tell you what, Jade. I suffer because you decided you didn't want me anymore. Life is the ultimate source of my pain, but you were all the happiness I have ever known. So I will forgive you. I will even give the world a reprieve."

"What are you asking of me?" said Jade.

Declan stood and held out a hand. The force binding Jade fell away. Hands finally free, Jade at first fell slack to the rocky ground. She made herself stand, though her joints were sore and stiff from the hours she and Rucksack had been bound and tormented. For a moment she wondered if the sky looked lighter, if the endless night was finally giving way to dawn.

"It's simple, of course, as these things are," said Declan. "Come back to me. Be with me, as you once were. Say yes to my question. I will be with you, kind and loving, for all your life."

"You'll spare the world? Stop trying to destroy all life?"

Declan shrugged. "Yes," he said. "For the duration of your life. I will give the world a little longer to live. The day you die is the day the world dies." His eyes narrowed, and his voice grew cold as he drew close to her again. "Whether that day is now or in the future, though, is up to you. Right now."

20

CHOICE

"You were kind, then," said Jade, hands by her side, palms tucked a little behind her legs. "Remember our first date?"

"We rode the ferry from Hong Kong Island to Kowloon and back," said Declan. A new smile came to him now. Not of cruelty, but of the simple joy of a fond memory. At least his face looked less grim. "You once told me that sometimes people treated you like this ugly shadow. But I remember how you looked in the sunshine that day. You shone."

Jade couldn't help but smile. It had been a rare kindness, a gleam in the dark that she could find her way by. For years after that day, Declan had been that light. And more than she had ever realized, she had been his too.

Until she had snuffed it out.

The guilt pulled at her. The guilt of leaving. The guilt of seeing now what he had become, the choices that he had made. He had been a good man. Flawed, but good. But now he was this. The gentle glow of years past, of love from long ago, faded like the sun setting into night.

"I wish you could be that man again," said Jade.

Declan shrugged. "I became who I am," he replied. "I lost my destiny, but I also learned that I don't need one. I found something better instead. I didn't need the world to tell me my way. I could find my own."

"This isn't how you had to be, though." Jade shook her head. "It was only a matter of time, Declan," she said. "Guess it might as well have been then."

The smile faded from Declan's face.

"You know why I made a different choice? Why I chose to leave?" Jade took a step toward him, careful to keep her hands hidden. She also circled around him, until her back was to the east. His gaze followed her every step, but he did not move, other than to remain facing her. "Deep down, maybe I always knew there was something wrong. Something cracked in you. Something that maybe you could fix, maybe you could change, but you had to want to. And you didn't want to. We weren't going to work out. What you are now... what happened... if it hadn't been me that you could blame this on, it would've been something else. Some other excuse. You didn't have to be this way. Something incredible happened to you. It could have been amazing. Instead, you chose to make it horrible."

Declan looked as if she had punched him. He took a step back. Rage, sadness, disappointment, heartbreak, confusion—all rushed through his eyes, swirling and fighting.

"You meant well with me," said Jade. "If we weren't going to work out, then it might as well have been that day in Hong Kong. But the rest? That's not on me. That was all you." She stood to her full height. She still might have been shorter than Declan was, but that didn't matter. She locked her gaze to his. "So there you go. No, I won't be with you. Because someone worth being with wouldn't do the things you want to do. Someone worth being with wouldn't force someone into the sort of choice you are forcing on me. But I'll tell you what. You think you're powerful? You want to kill me?" She leaned forward. "Then you'd better be tough enough to look me in the eye when you do it."

His face was less dark now. Finally. Around them, the sky lightened. From some faraway crag or valley, Jade was certain she heard a bird chirp.

Then, though she couldn't see it, she could feel the sky changing, the world waking. From over the mountains ringing them to the east, the sun emerged.

Like a spear, a ray of sunlight beamed over the mountains, across the plain—and into Declan's eyes. He yelped and covered his face.

Finally, Jade raised one of her hands. And threw the rock she had picked up as she stood.

The rock cracked Declan's forehead and knocked his head back.

Rucksack leaped to his feet, fully healed. Jade wondered how long he had been lying there, motionless yet awake, waiting. She threw the other rock, but Declan ducked it. A force flowed from him that knocked Jade and Rucksack off their feet.

"So you've chosen," said Declan.

Jade looked away. She couldn't stand again. The sun continued rising, but Declan had managed to restrain Jade and Rucksack again. She struggled against him, tried to break free so she could move again, but she couldn't. Disappointment flooded her now, along with the frustration that she had failed to stop him. And she was furious with The Management. They had known. All this time they had known. They could have told her. But they didn't. Because they needed her to keep going, to get there, to believe only that she was a chosen one, special. There to stop the villain and save the world.

"I always regretted what happened to you," said Rucksack softly. "It didn't have to be this way. None o' it did."

"I'm going to kill you now," said Declan, his voice flat and distant. "First Rucksack." He looked from the hero to the ex. "Then you." He smiled. "Then the world."

He raised his hands. Then stopped. "No." Declan turned to

face Jade. "First you die," said Declan. "Rucksack, I want you to see the end result of that day. First I want you to see your friend, the person you should have told the truth to, die. I want you to wonder what would have happened if only you had told her everything."

The pain built up in Declan's eyes, but with it came the fury. Whatever he could control, Jade sensed it was all from pain and agony. All that evil came from pain. She remembered one of her teachers telling her that. Not that the training would matter anymore now.

She looked Declan in the eye. "You could have been so much more."

Declan sneered. "This will do."

He raised his hands. Despite the sunlight brightening a new day, Jade could feel the world grow silent and cold. Within moments, the fire would come. Within moments, silence and cold would be all that she knew.

21

EXHALE

 ailed.

All the striving, all the hardship, all the hope, all burned to ashes in the fury of Jade's heart. Then the sadness came, tall crashing waves that snuffed out the angry flames. The Management had been wrong to send her. She couldn't stop Declan after all.

She couldn't be with him. No chance. While she could use his feelings against him, he was beyond feelings. He was too powerful now. She gave up trying to struggle against the power holding her body still.

In the world beyond Jade's closed eyes, a heat grew. The power was drawing near. She wondered if death would be fast or slow, agonizing or painless. Not that it mattered too much. The end would be the same.

Declan could control her body, but he could not control her thoughts. Jade tried to focus on the Heart of the World, on her training, on her hope, on anything. There had to be something, here at the end, that she could do. Something that could protect the people inside—and barricade the hidden power within. Something that could keep Declan from taking the power he sought and ending all life.

One last time, Jade breathed in. A roar filled the air, like the sky before a tornado touches down.

Then it came.

Death must begin with ruptured eardrums. The sound was unbearable now. The roar took away every other sound Jade had known.

Then the sound changed. The roar fell away—and Declan began screaming.

Jade opened her eyes.

And realized she could move.

Declan was staggering backward and in erratic, weaving circles. He held a hand to his head, and blood streamed down his face while he roared in pain. On the ground near his feet, a rock the size of a grapefruit rolled and wobbled and finally became still.

Jade glanced up. The rock that had hit Declan in the head must have fallen from somewhere off the mountain. A bit of chance had bought her and Rucksack precious moments. Jade looked around and realized she had no idea what to do with that little bit of time. There was no defeating Declan. He was too powerful.

Declan stopped staggering around.

The moments were almost gone. Declan pulled his bloody hand from his head and held it out toward Jade. The wildness still blazed in his eyes, but his cold fury was starting to tame it.

But the hand was farther away now. So was Declan. So was the ground.

Jade looked back. Rucksack was a little above her and had wrapped an arm around her waist. They were flying faster now, going up the mountainside, rising with the sun. Declan yelled again, frustrated and furious.

"How did you figure it out?" asked Jade.

Declan was far below them now, too far away to hurt them. Even his roars and screams were getting faint.

"Being about to die is a great reminder that everything else is a matter o' perspective," said Rucksack. "Now it's your turn."

He let her go.

Her eyes widened. She waited for the plunge—but she did not fall.

"It makes sense now," said Jade, flying up so that she and Rucksack were side by side. "Lightness of spirit," she continued. "No matter our guilt and pain, we have a reason to live."

"Exactly," said Rucksack. "We couldn't defeat Declan—this time."

Jade grinned. "Now there can be a next time. And we'll be ready."

"We had no idea what we were facing," said Rucksack. "I knew what had happened to Declan in Hong Kong, and no, I didn't want to tell you. But I didn't know he was here, not any more than you did."

"I believe you," said Jade, the words dry yet sincere in the thin air. They were high up the mountain now. Below, Declan was a mere speck. Before them, the eastern slope of the Heart of the World glowed silver and gold in the early sunlight.

"Guilt and pain for many things can weigh me down," said Rucksack. "No matter my own guilt and pain, though, I have a reason to live. I'm still here to protect the world, and right now that means protecting the Heart o' the World. I need to help stop Declan. And I will."

"We made our choices," said Jade. "They affected Declan. But we didn't make him this way."

"Above all, he's not all-powerful or invulnerable," added Rucksack. "We nearly had him earlier, and that rock conked him good just now. A little more and he would have been out."

"His power is all based in pain and fury," said Jade. "We can use that. He is wounded and broken. He finds strength there. Fair enough. It's still a strength he uses for terrible things—and it's more limited than he realizes. We can figure out his weaknesses and stop him. Especially before Declan can break into the mountain and harm the people there. I know they're powerful…" Jade trailed off, unable to say the rest.

"But they won't be able to defeat him," said Rucksack, though it was hard for him to say the words. "I know."

"We need a strategy," said Jade.

Rucksack smiled. "I know where we can make one."

Rucksack flew faster, and Jade kept pace. She looked ahead, beyond the mountain, to the cloud fortress floating above.

They flew toward the top of the mountain. Jade knew that Declan would redouble his efforts, fueled by fury and frustration. Now that she and Rucksack had escaped, he'd be even angrier. He'd be even more dangerous. But she and Rucksack would be ready. Over the summit they flew now. From here the world was little pieces—toy mountains and blue marker lines of rivers. Across the world, in the rising morning sun, bright greens stretched in the light. There would be people in villages, animals living their lives. Forests rising high.

And Declan wanted to end it all. He could see only his pain, and nothing beyond.

For now, though, Jade gloried in still having a heartbeat, and in the wider world laid out before her. Beyond her and Rucksack, the world was heading to a sunrise full of golds and silvers. Yes, Declan would be waiting. Yes, the world was in danger. But for a moment, Jade and Rucksack were flying, and the joy of that glorious freedom filled her from soul to bone. Passing across the summit, Jade looked east. Between the sun above and world below, she glanced south too. Somewhere was Agamuskara. Somewhere, the Everest Base Camp still waited for her. If only she could find her way through this.

They passed over the center of the summit, and Jade looked down. She could see only the broken, jagged, teeth-like brown shards, charred black at the edges, that ringed the mountaintop like a crown. She wondered what the explosion must have been like, when the mountain had blown. How far away could people see the blast? Feel it? How long did the ash and smoke, the fire and molten rock, leave their mark on the world? What life suffered and ended because of the explosion?

Now, though, the magma chamber was empty. The mountain was hollow inside, and Jade could see far, far down into it. When the sun was at its zenith, Jade wondered if she'd be able to see all the way down to the bottom.

She also wondered if she'd still feel the disquiet that she felt now. Something about the Heart didn't make sense, but she didn't know what. She tried to look deeper, tried to figure it out—

"Jade!"

Jade looked to Rucksack, then followed his pointing left arm. They passed beyond the summit, between mountain and cloud. Arcing upward, they neared the bottom of the cloud fortress.

"We're almost there," said Rucksack.

Jade smiled. Even in the morning light the cloud fortress was a matte, stormish gray. But Jade knew that was all part of the brilliance: camouflage the amazing in the dull. Outside, it was flat gray wisps. But inside—Jade could all but see it now—a new world waited.

PART III

22

———

INSIDE

Jade and Rucksack passed through the outer concealing wall of cloud. Jade, not wanting to miss a moment, forced her eyes to stay open. The sunlight followed them through the wall. It shone out over the top of the cloud fortress and lit up the new world before them.

Building the cloud fortress so that it looked like the Heart of the World, only upside down, Rucksack had given himself a canvas the size of a small city. From the broad top of the cloud, some spheres, cubes, and pyramids pushed into the sky like buildings. They dazzled in oranges, peaches, golds, and silvery grays. Jade could make out rectangles and circles on structures—windows. They even had some sort of panes in them, but surely there wasn't glass up here?

Between the buildings ran broad lanes, empty and straight, north to south and east to west. A diagonal street ran northeast to southwest, and another ran northwest to southeast. From the edge to the center, the buildings and lanes were arranged in a series of concentric circles. At the center, an empty, open plaza led to a main structure in the center. This structure was not like the others. It was mountain-shaped like the Heart of the World far below, only smaller, more human-scale. In the sunlight it glowed gold and silver, a shining heart in the morning.

Rucksack took her hand. He guided Jade toward what looked like a flat disc—a sort of platform—near the outer edge of the city. They lowered, hovering, floating slowly downward now.

Would it actually hold them? Jade tried to keep her heart light, tried not to doubt. They had come this far. Then her feet touched something solid. Jade let go of the lightness of flight, and her body's weight return to her. She touched down on the flat gray cloud.

The cloud held, and she stood.

"Welcome to my finest cloud fortress," said Rucksack, standing to her left. "My flagship." He raised his left arm and swept it around the shapes and vistas before them. "May I show you around?"

Jade nodded. The buildings grew from the cloud like trees from a forest floor, like the mountains from the earth below. The lanes were straight, the curves of the concentric circles elegant and proportional. "All this," she said. "From cloud."

"The cloud is the culmination o' all elements: water, earth, fire, and wind," said Rucksack. "That's why I chose it. Cloud seems soft but it can endure, as long as you know how to work with it, shape it, understand it."

They began walking northwest, toward the center, on the empty diagonal street. The mountain-shaped citadel at the heart of the cloud fortress rose.

The strange thing about walking on cloud was that as solid as it was, your footsteps were always silent. There was always a slight spring to the surface, as if the street were helping you walk.

"The windows are wisp thin, and like the doors they open with a thought," continued Rucksack.

"How do you have windows here?" said Jade.

"You can forge and hammer gold until it's an atom thick,"

replied Rucksack. "Cloud is similar. Those windows are as thin as a hair, but harder than glass. All made o' cloud."

"It's like the place is listening to us," said Jade. "But it's empty, right?"

"Yes," said Rucksack. "We're the first people to set foot here in five hundred years. And you're right. In a sense the fortress can listen. It can respond to our breath and thought. Cloud is soft and formable, yet the walls are harder than steel." He smiled. "I built my cloud fortresses to endure."

All around them, Jade could see the truth in his words. Despite being empty for so long, there was no sign of wear or neglect. No tumbled ruins blocked the graceful circular lanes. No building ended in jagged shards. It was as if construction had just finished.

"A union of nature and imagination," said Jade. She looked at Rucksack and smiled. "It also says a lot about you."

"What do you mean?"

"That inside there is a man of love and beauty," she said. "A man of resilience and strength. Only someone full of love and kindness could create something enduring and beautiful from something so fleeting."

"That's possibly the kindest thing anyone has ever said to me," said Rucksack. "Thank you."

For a time they walked in silence, and Jade's smile faded. The cloud fortress was amazing, and she wanted to run through the streets like a little girl. But she couldn't. There was still much to do—and many things to know. "Which makes it all the more important," continued Jade, "that you tell me the rest of the truth."

"I haven't lied to you."

"Never said you had," replied Jade. "But you've been a bit over-selective with what you share."

"You want to know what else I know about you and Declan."

Jade didn't need to reply.

"The day you made your choice, something in him broke," said Rucksack. "Part o' that is my fault. His memories were fading. Even from where I stood, seven stories up, on top o' that white pagoda in the Gardens, I could see it in his eyes." He shook his head. "I had returned something to its... well, not owner, for no one can own it, but its holder. A little stone. Well, more than a stone, but that's another story for another time. It fell from the pagoda and landed in front o' Declan. When Declan picked it up, when he looked up and saw me and Jake Hongkong up there, it caught him at the right moment. He held on to his memories."

"He had to hold in his head two things," said Jade. "Both what he was supposed to know of me now that I had chosen to become a Jade, and what he already knew of our time together."

"Yes," said Rucksack. "I tried to follow him. Tried to talk to him. It could be I shouldn't have. I've often wondered if that's what pushed him over. He had a love for you, Jade. I don't doubt that, and I don't think you do either. But something in that love... inverted. Changed. The pain o' what had happened broke him. Afterward, he made his way to the pub where he had been earlier."

"The Management won't speak of this," said Jade. "None of us know what happened in the Hong Kong Incident."

"Declan didn't mean to do it. He didn't mean to shoot Jake." Rucksack shook his head. "But those damn elixirs you Jakes and Jades keep, so you can muck with people's destinies and decisions? Declan drank enough o' one that it stripped away his own destiny. It's like his present poisoned his future, Jade. He didn't know it would happen. Neither did I, or Jake, and I doubt any being ever could've guessed."

"You couldn't stop it?"

"I couldn't get inside." Rucksack sighed. "The Management had figured out that I was in Hong Kong, and they did something to keep me from going back inside the pub. Later, I was able to; in the chaos o' what happened, I figure they let their little lock slip. I don't know. But when Declan left the pub, I tried again to stop him, reason with him, help him. He knocked me out cold, Jade. Even then, his pain was giving him strength. When I came to, he was gone, and I hadn't seen him since. I've looked for him. So many places I've been over the years, but there hasn't been a peep about Declan. It was as if he was a ghost that had vanished in the dawn. Nothing at all. Until you and I happened upon him yesterday."

"I wish you had told me this," said Jade. "I wish you had given me the chance to understand. I don't know if it would have made a difference or not, but I deserved to know."

"You did," said Rucksack. "I didn't tell you because I felt ashamed o' what happened. Not because o' you."

"Then that's the crux of it," said Jade. Her voice was hard but she was certain Rucksack could hear the cracks in it. "This is going to be the difference between us and Declan. He has only his pain. We have each other." She held out her hand. "Friends can hurt each other, but we also can forgive. We can rely on each other, no matter what."

Rucksack shook her hand. "Thank you," he said, "though such friendship and forgiveness are more than I deserve."

"I'm giving you a pass." Jade smiled. "On account of your artistic vision." She gave his hand a squeeze. "But don't do it again."

"I'll tell you all I can," said Rucksack.

"I can handle it," said Jade. "All ten thousand years, if need be."

They continued on. At the heart of the cloud fortress, the citadel glowed silver and gold in the morning light. "That was my refuge in my refuge," said Rucksack. "My own little hidey-hole in the sky. Even heroes sometimes need to kick back on their own with a quiet beer."

"Why did you make the place so big?" asked Jade. "If it's only for you, I mean sure, the place is as big as the biggest mountain, but isn't it a bit much?"

Rucksack smiled. "O' course it's a bit much. I wanted to see how much I could do," he said. "But it's more than that. I built this cloud fortress as a refuge and safe haven for those in need."

"How would you have done that?" asked Jade. "If you are all about being in the background, that doesn't exactly work when you put thousands of people on a cloud. That sort of thing tends to stick in someone's mind. Not to mention, how would you get them up here, if the only way up is to fly?"

"Oh, a cloud fortress floats," said Rucksack.

"But you can land it too."

Rucksack nodded. "That's part o' why I want us to go to the citadel," said Rucksack. "Like I told you, my memory o' many things has been spotty at best since The Blast. I remember more now, but holes remain. I have something in the citadel. A forgetting stone that my grandparents helped me make. If I had to bring people here, then later they could leave with no memory o' me or this place. It would protect me, and it protects them too. The world is better off with me behind the scenes, Jade, and above all with no one knowing I'm there."

She nodded. "The price of being different." Then she glanced away, not sure why.

It had to have been from one of the windows in a spherical building nearby. She was certain of it, but there was no way.

Yet it had to have been a flicker of movement. She stopped. All the wonder of the cloud fortress, all the comfort of knowing she had a stalwart friend, it all faded away.

She leaned toward Rucksack. "We're being watched."

"Impossible," he replied. "There's no one here, Jade. No one but me ever knew about the cloud fortresses. Even if someone happened to figure it out, it's not exactly everybody who can fly. You and I are the only people here."

Jade said nothing more, and they continued on again. The

citadel was close now. Still, Jade found herself looking for any other movement, the slightest hint of motion. But all was still. The cloud city was massive, beautiful—but empty.

The doors of the citadel glowed golden in the sunlight, with little motifs in brown and black. No, not motifs, she realized.

"Languages," said Jade, touching the door.

The solid cloud looked like painted wood. Even in its solidity the door held a sense of resistance and intangibility, both there yet not there at the same time. Writing covered the door and its frame. "Is there any human language not represented here?"

"No," said Rucksack. "I never knew who might need to be here, so I figured I should give them all the same message."

Jade nodded. "All who need help and refuge," she read. "Welcome."

"A citadel isn't exactly known for being the most welcoming o' places," said Rucksack.

"But for a warrior and a hero," said Jade, "you aren't exactly about doing anything typical or expected."

"That's the thing about all the heroing," said Rucksack. "Like you, Jade, I'd rather see change than defeat."

"Maybe that's where we went wrong down there with Declan," said Jade.

"We rushed in, without thought, and everything went wrong." Rucksack shook his head. "Fighting always seems so easy, so simple, so straightforward. You see it in the stories. People always expect it to be the big battle, the big brawl that decides all things."

"All that did was nearly get us killed," said Jade. "Maybe the best hero isn't the one with the best fighting moves."

"The best hero is the one who doesn't need them," replied Rucksack.

"Is that what you are? The best hero?"

Rucksack shrugged. "I've been in more than my share o' scraps," he said. "But I try, Jade Bluegold. I try. Maybe one day."

"How does the door open?"

"Two keys, so to speak," said Rucksack. "Only me, my parents, or my grandparents could unlock these doors, so one o' us had to be here for the door to want to open. I'm here, so that's step one."

"Step two?"

"Ask. In your mind, ask the door to open. As long as I'm on the fortress and hold the yes in my mind, the door will open."

Jade did. Instead of swinging inward or sliding into the walls, the golden doors faded, like cloud changing as it moved in a high wind. Jade and Rucksack stepped inside. Jade glanced back to see the doors reform.

The silence in the citadel seemed different than outside. Maybe it was the idea of being inside a building made of cloud. Maybe it was the low dark ceiling, the same brown and black as Rucksack's eyes. Despite the low, cavernous feel to the citadel, it was bright.

"Sunlight, starlight, moonlight, they all filter through the cloud," said Rucksack. "There is always light here."

"I can't figure it out," said Jade. "This space... doesn't quite trouble me, but it's so different. It's like this silence... is lived in, you know? Like a closed room where someone has been for a long time."

"The ventilation is excellent, if I do say so myself," said Rucksack. "But it has been shut up awhile nonetheless."

They came to a circular wall. "There's a door at each compass point," said Rucksack. "We need to head to the center o' the room. That's where I kept the forgetting stone."

They found a door and went inside. Here, the room was black as well, but accented with golds and silvers. At the center of the room, a hole in the ceiling let in a shaft of sunlight. It shone on a short, narrow white column, waist high to Jade. They stood at the column—but no black stone was there.

"It should be here," said Rucksack. Worry flooded his voice

and his face. "It was there when last I was here. He glanced around. "It's egg shaped, and about the size o' a tumbler. Maybe it fell."

They were about to start searching for it, when the sound of doors opening made them turn. All four doors were open now, and people were streaming into the room at the heart of the citadel. Dozens and dozens, faces smooth and worn, bodies short and tall, slender and broad. Women and men of all ages, but no children. Their skin shone brown in the golden sunlight, reminding Jade of the hills and mountains she had spent the past weeks trekking through.

When all the people had come inside, they closed the doors behind them. They surrounded Jade and Rucksack in an unbroken circle.

"Rucksack," said Jade, "maybe more people knew about this place than you thought."

23

VISIT

Rucksack and Jade stood back to back and turned slowly, staring at the dozens of people around them. No one moved forward. No one spoke. All wore simple but well-made clothes: creamy whites and earthy browns. The color of their skin ranged from dark to pale. No one appeared hurt or malnourished. They were of heaven and earth, with the ethereal glow to their skin and eyes coexisting with an earthiness. Jade could see kindness and intelligence in their eyes. Their rough calloused hands clearly knew what it meant to work with land, plants, animals. They looked like the kind of people who could discuss the highest philosophies of life—then tell jokes that would make nuns and sailors blush.

"Who are you?" asked Rucksack. "And what are you doing on my cloud?"

Before them, people began to shift, forming an opening. Two people walked through: a man and a woman. They looked older, could pass for senior citizens in the outer world. Yet a power and vitality flowed from them. Jade could feel it even across the room. They wore long pants and long-sleeved, tunic-like long shirts over the pants. Simple yet intricate designs of whites, silvers, golds, and grays wove through the fabric.

The color fell out of Rucksack's face. "I didn't remember," he said. "I'm sorry... O' course... O' course you are..." Jade could hear the fear in his voice, the fear of rejection and condemnation.

The woman and the man came to Rucksack.

And embraced him.

"*Mola*," said Rucksack in Tibetan. "*Pola.*"

Jade's eyes widened, as her training translated the words. Grandmother. Grandfather.

"*Dbon po*," they said back.

Grandson.

She looked around the room. The people of the Heart of the World weren't in the mountain.

They were right here.

"You had nothing to fear," said Rucksack's grandmother.

"We forgive you," said his grandfather.

"For The Blast?" said Rucksack. "But how? But what about Mother?"

"Because you are our dbon po," said Rucksack's grandmother. "Because you are trying to make things right."

"Our daughter made her choice," said his grandfather. "Even at the end, she believed in you. So do we. You are always welcome at the Heart of the World."

"Thank you," said Rucksack. He took a step back. "My friend, Jade Agamuskara Bluegold."

Jade bowed her head. "It's an honor to meet you," she said. Yet as she spoke she felt a tug of memory, something she couldn't place, but it was there, a little splinter in her mind. It wasn't from Rucksack's grandparents. It was from seeing the other people in the room.

"It is an honor to know you," said Rucksack's grandmother. "We have a rule in the Heart of the World. Our true names are only for ourselves. So, you may call us Mola and Pola, as Rucksack does."

Jade didn't know what to say.

"You did not know your grandparents well, did you, child?" said Pola.

"No," said Jade. "My... The people I grew up with... I didn't see much of anyone."

The tug pulled harder. A cold wind blew through a hole in her heart. Jade knew, deep in her bones and soul, that she had missed out on something in her life that she should not have missed.

"We have seen so much," said Mola. "We saw your train, Jade, and we saw the village and some of your journey here. We saw Declan and what happened at the base of our mountain."

Bitterness struck through Jade like lightning. "If you'd done all that seeing, it's a shame you couldn't have done something to help."

"As you can understand, we could not risk revealing ourselves to Declan," said Pola. "But that doesn't mean we didn't help."

Jade stared at them. Then understood.

The moments her eyes were closed, when death had seemed so certain.

"The rock," said Jade. "The rock that dazed him. You did that."

Mola nodded. "My aim isn't what it used to be. I didn't want to kill him, so you know. We avoid killing whenever possible, and hurt only if we must. But I had hoped to knock him out. That would have made things so much easier. I'm sorry it all went so hard for you."

"He tortured us. All night." Jade didn't bother keeping her voice even. Every heated word rose in frustration. Her eyes narrowed, and she clenched her fists. "You couldn't have chucked that rock earlier?"

"We tried," said Pola. "The powers that Declan wields, it was as if he had some sort of protection around the three of you. We showered rocks down—they all disintegrated. We even looked at using the cloud fortress's defenses, but there was no way we could be certain of missing you. I'm sorry."

"He nearly killed us," said Jade.

"But he didn't," said Mola. "I know it's not enough. But it's what is."

"Much of our lives have been like this of late," said Pola. "We have watched. We have helped some too, though in ways that has helped us stay obscured and unknown."

"I don't understand," said Rucksack. "You were in the mountain. You've been in the Heart o' the World since before I was born."

Mola touched her grandson's face. "You really don't remember?"

Rucksack shook his head.

"We told you that you did a fine job crafting the forgetting stone," said Pola, and he smiled with a grandfather's pride.

"How long have you been here?" asked Rucksack.

"About five hundred years now," said Mola. "We have been both apart from the world yet also some part of the world."

"We've been trying to help where we can," said Pola. "We've been trying to do some right in the world. I suppose you could say we've been trying to seed some light and goodness, and see what takes root in people."

"Five hundred years," said Jade. "You saw The Blast."

"That is not something we could have stopped," said Mola.

"But what happened after..." Jade's voice trailed off for a moment as she recollected. "It's been said that more should have died. That for all the horror and destruction, it was miraculous that so many survived."

Rucksack's grandparents said nothing. Jade looked from them to the people circling the room. "You all helped, didn't you?"

No one said anything, but Jade understood the answer anyway. "And afterward," she continued. "Bloodless revolutions in places like Ireland, Scotland, and India—they regained their independence with hardly a drop of blood spilled. Did you do that?"

"Not directly," said Mola. "We do not direct. We guide. People must make their own choices."

Pola smiled. "But that doesn't mean we didn't give some nudges here and there," he said. "We helped people who went on to become, shall we say, pivotal in those movements."

"You've been helping all over the world, all this time?" said Jade.

"Yes," said Mola. "Some years back, we even found ourselves over Vancouver Island." She motioned to a woman, who took a step forward.

Jade gasped. Her memory stopped tugging at her. She knew now why seeing the group of people had pulled at her. It wasn't the group. It was this one woman.

The day she ran away. The woman who had let her on to the ferry.

"The greatest kindnesses are the small levers that move and change the world," said Pola.

"Call me Taras," said the woman. The Sanskrit word for ferry, Jade understood.

"Call me grateful," said Jade. She approached and stood before the woman who had changed her life. Jade bowed low. "Thank you," she said. "The day I ran away... every moment in my life since has been because of your grace and kindness."

Taras took Jade's hands. "Your life knew much that a child should not know," said Taras. "You needed a second chance."

"I hope I've done it justice," said Jade.

"You have," replied Taras. "You've paid it forward at every opportunity. The chance I gave you, you have returned in multitudes. And will continue to, in ways you do not yet know."

The tears came down Jade's face then, and Taras folded Jade into her arms. The scent of fresh-baked bread came to Jade. So did the touch of sun-warmed earth and the sound of waves knocking against the hull of a boat as it crossed a sea.

"I will help Rucksack protect you," said Jade. "All of you. The Heart of the World. This fortress. All I am is because of the chance you gave me. I will repay your kindness, now and always."

Taras kissed her forehead. Jade returned to where Rucksack stood with his grandparents.

"We have tried to help where we can," said Mola. "But it has not been enough. We have not succeeded yet in helping the world regain its hope, or regain its desire for love over power. Saving the world isn't a spectator sport. The only way to help the world is to be among the world."

"Why not return?" said Jade.

Pola shrugged. "Why have The Management never revealed the Jakes and Jades?"

Jade nodded. "Because there is still much fear in the world."

"We see the despair, but we see hope too," said Mola. "We see it more than ever. We have seen peace. We have seen change. There are signs that, someday, someday, we may be able to return after all."

Mola touched Jade's face. "I see all those things, right here, with you, child. I am grateful you found my grandson. You are a sign of hope beyond what I ever could have dreamed."

"We would like to be among people again," said Pola. "But first we have to deal with Declan and the threat he faces. If we survive that, if the world survives, then we would like to see when we can return to the world. We long to be among people and to work together again, as we once did."

"First we must understand, though," said Rucksack. "How did you come to be here to begin with?"

Mola asked for people to bring food and drink. "Please sit," she told Jade and Rucksack.

"But Declan?" said Jade.

"What you need to hear will also help us against him," said Pola. "Plus, you are weary. Sit, and first we'll tell you a story." He smiled at his grandson. "A story, my dbon po, about how you brought us here."

24

———

STORY

Some of the people of the Heart brought in food—*balep* bread, oranges, fried pies, butter tea—and bottles of stout. Jade smiled. Even here, above the roof of the world, at least they could get a decent pint.

And Jade couldn't deny it: sitting down felt so good. Even with her healing, the last couple of days had pushed her weary body beyond its limits. Resting on couches made of dark cloud, Jade could feel her body begin to heal from Declan's torment.

Mola herself brought Jade a plate of food and a pint of black beer. The plate had a wispy, swirled design, and was dark gray. The pint glass seemed made of spun threads. While not completely clear, the translucent glass showed the dark beer and its pillowy, snowy white head.

"Are the plates made of cloud too?" asked Jade.

"Aye, but the glasses are the hard part, like the windows," said Rucksack. "You have to be able to forge the cloud so it is thin but not brittle, and the curves are surprisingly tricky. I've not yet been able to craft a clear one. Who knows, someday I can try again. You know, if the world calms down a bit."

Once everyone had food and drink, Rucksack looked at his

grandparents. "I have no memory o' bringing you here," he said. "And five hundred years ago... the most notable thing I recall is going to the top o' Mount Everest to check something. I don't remember anything about coming to the Heart o' the World. Though now that I think about it, it's strange that I would come so close and then not come see you."

Mola and Pola smiled. "Five hundred years ago, you came for a visit," said Mola, "but it was a dark time here. You did not know it yet, and centuries had passed since your last visit."

"We have lived in the Heart of the World for tens of thousands of years," said Pola. "We had begun to despair that we would never leave. We have wonderful things there, Jade. We have learned to grow all sorts of crops. Everything you are eating right now, even the oranges, came from our farms and greenhouses inside the mountain. We can pasture animals, make cheese, craft things from the minerals and ore we mine."

"And inside the mountain isn't dark," added Mola. "We've crafted the surface of the mountain. Light shines through, yet you cannot tell from outside."

"What about the beer?" Jade asked.

"As you can imagine, First Call Brewing doesn't exactly deliver out here," said Mola. "Even if they did, we would not want to risk drawing Guru Deep's attention to our existence."

"No indeed," said Rucksack.

"We brew our own beer," said Pola, "with barley we grow and malt, and our own hops. It's not quite Galway Pradesh Stout, as you know it in the wider world. But since our daughter helped invent it, we hope it's close enough to do her proud."

The mention of Rucksack's mother made him wince. His grandmother tapped his knee with her palm.

"When you came here," said Mola, "you thought you were visiting family, having a bit of a reunion. But when you came through the eastern gate, you saw a different Heart than the one you had last seen. We were ill. Not from sickness but from despair. We were beginning to think we had been wrong, that the people of the world would forever choose power over love. We would have no place in such a world. Yet as we realized how long we would have to endure in the mountain..." As she shook her head, sadness sat heavy in her eyes.

"We wanted sunshine again, and to smell the sea," Mola continued. "We wanted to see the world beyond our mountain walls again, but we feared we never would."

"We told you our despair, my dbon po," said Pola. "You told us you would help us, your family, the people of the Heart, the people who had trained you and looked out for you. You understood that we had hidden away for too long. We had seen nothing of the changes of the world, and knew too little of it. You climbed to the top of the mountain. For three days you sat there thinking, deliberating, feeling our pain as your own."

"Then, one morning, the wind blew fiercely, so fiercely that we feared for you," said Mola. "We thought that the wind might knock you from the mountain to your death. So Pola and I came up to bring you down. Clouds had covered the top of the mountain and we could barely see. When we found you, you stood in greeting. Then the wind died down. You smiled at us, then you reached out and grabbed a piece of cloud."

Pola chuckled. "You began to spin it like wool into yarn. You told us you knew what you would do."

"It took months, and you did not leave the top of the mountain that entire time," said Mola. "When you finished the cloud fortress, you flew it to the ground, then you led us out of the eastern gate. It was the first time in tens of thousands of years that we had passed through that door. The cloud fortress glowed gold and silver in the morning sun, and we were amazed at what you had done for us."

"In flight we followed you here," said Pola. "You showed us everything we needed to know, how to pilot the fortress, how to observe the world from it, how to use its systems."

With a grin, Mola stood. "You even taught us where we could fly down from it, and be as much a part of the world as we could and wanted."

With a chuckle, Jade stared at them. "You fly down from the sky and help people in need," she said. "Many cultures tell tales of beings who do that. They're called angels."

Mola smiled. And winked.

"Dbon po, you gave us more than a refuge," said Pola, standing next to his wife and holding her hand. "You gave us a new home. Yet even that was not all. You gave us hope. We did not feel we could return to the world yet. But we could at least see the world, observe it, make decisions with new information. And we could help where we could. As we did, we began to see that all was not wickedness. There was kindness too." Pola smiled. "With a little help, that kindness could grow. Someday it might overtake the evil."

Rucksack shook his head. "I did all this, yet remember none o' it."

Mola and Pola held out their joined hands, then opened them. Lying on their palms rested the black, egg-shaped forgetting stone.

"Because you also made this," said Mola. "We told you it wasn't necessary, but you insisted. You said you wanted us to be safe and to be free. You knew the dangers you faced. You feared that something might happen to you that could compromise us. Much harm could come to us and the world if we were found out, or if some evil learned about the cloud fortress. So you chose to forget what you had done. You said it was the greatest protection you could give us. You told us you would only return when circumstance brought you here. When you did return, it would mark the beginning of great change for us all."

Pola smiled. "My dbon po, that time has come. Touch the stone again. Just as saying good-bye will trigger the stone's forgetting power, ask to remember. The stone will restore your memory."

Rucksack laid his hand on the stone and closed his eyes. In the passing moments, every person was silent.

Rucksack's eyes opened wide. Jade could all but see the memories returning—flashes and images amidst the fire of his dark eyes.

A glow went through the room—gratitude and the love of family. Jade looked around at the people of the Heart.

Rucksack smiled. "I remember," he said. "It worked. I don't mean the stone... rather, it worked... but... you. The plan. It worked. You're here. You're okay."

"Your kindness restored our hope," said Mola.

Rucksack held the forgetting stone. He opened his mouth to say more. Jade, too, had much to say: about the stone, about the fortress, about the threat below.

Then the cloud fortress shook. All the people of the Heart of the World doubled over, crying out in sudden, intense pain.

"What's going on?" said Jade.

"They are connected to their mountain home," said Rucksack as he helped his grandparents up. "That pain can only mean one thing."

Mola nodded, her face grim and sad. "Yes," she said. "Declan has broken through into the Heart of the World."

25

PLAN

Jade, Rucksack, and the others stood at the western edge of the cloud fortress and looked down. Rubble covered the area where, a day ago, Declan had almost killed her and Rucksack. Now a hole gaped in the mountain, as if it had grown a mouth.

The people of the Heart still trembled with pain, but they were moving now. Everyone was trying to figure out what to do. Jade didn't want to say anything. She realized now that Mola, Pola, and the others had never expected Declan to succeed. No one had said it, but Jade could see it in their eyes. It was in the way they looked away from her—a hint of embarrassment.

They'd underestimated the enemy. And now realized how bad a mistake that had been.

They all looked down over the edge, expecting to see nothing but the rock. Yet there was Declan. He stood completely still, eyes closed, as if sleeping standing up. The energy expenditure had weakened him, but he was restoring himself. Recharging, so that when he went inside, he would be as powerful as possible.

Jade wondered if he had known he would succeed, or if Declan was as surprised as the People of the Heart.

Around Declan the air shimmered. For now he was still completely protected. He was wary, she was sure, of the two enemies who he knew were still around somewhere.

Sooner or later, though, he would wake. As soon as he did he would go into the Heart of the World. He would find the force at the heart of the Heart, dominate it, wield it, take the power of the world itself as if it were his own. Jade looked to the ragged top of the mountain. She wondered what the eruption would look like. How quickly it would destroy them, and how long Declan would take to eradicate life from the world.

Jade could imagine him, wandering an empty, silent, gray, dead world.

She wondered if he would actually find the peace he sought. Or when he didn't, what he would turn his anger and agony toward next.

From there, she looked to the hole in the Heart. Then she nodded toward Rucksack.

He stood with her. "Yes?"

"I think Declan's in some sort of... trance," said Jade. "I don't think he's very aware of the world right now. You said your cloud fortress has weapons, right?"

"O' course," he replied.

"Think you could knock that hole closed again?"

Rucksack shrugged. "Easy as grabbing a pint," he said. "But it won't stop him. And it might expose us."

Jade nodded. "That's a risk we have to take, and at the least we can slow him down. We need every moment we can wring out of this mess."

Rucksack turned to his grandparents, and they nodded. Rucksack left. A couple of minutes later, a silvery glow appeared from the underside of the cloud fortress. Jagged and thick, a bolt of lightning shot down. The hole at the base of the Heart of the World collapsed into a pile of rubble, blocking the way inside that Declan had blasted.

"We've got some time," said Jade. "Let's make it——"

Before she could finish, another bolt of lightning lashed out from the cloud fortress. This one struck down where Declan stood. A white flash, blinding and painful, blasted upward toward the cloud fortress. Jade stepped back, rubbing her eyes. When her vision cleared and she came back to the edge, she looked down, her heart thudding with hope.

The shield shimmered. Inside, Declan stood motionless, still recharging—and unharmed.

"Damn," said Jade.

Rucksack came back, looked down, and shrugged. "Well, it was worth a go."

Mola turned to the crowd before her. People came forward, nodding, as if they already knew what they would be expected to do. Mola's face was grim as she nodded. Without a word, the people turned and walked back toward the citadel at the center of the cloud fortress.

"Where are they going?" asked Jade.

"From the citadel, they can open the floor and fly down out of the cloud fortress," said Mola. "They are returning to the Heart of the World. They are going to do what they can. Declan is in our home. We know the mountain. He doesn't. We have defenses there. Perhaps they're enough to stop Declan." She shook her head. "All those who left are also mighty, and have mastered many forms of combat. At the least, they might buy us more time."

Mola tried to keep her voice steady, but Jade could hear how empty and hollow the words sounded.

Jade stared at the citadel. She started to ask if the people would come back, but she caught a glimpse of Mola's eyes. The despair there was answer enough.

Mola also assigned other people with the task of watching Declan and reporting any changes. Then she, Jade, Rucksack, Pola, and the others returned to the citadel. When they arrived, it was empty. Jade tried to find some hope for the people who had left, but instead found that they must have taken all the remaining hope with them.

Inside the citadel, Jade, Rucksack, Mola, Pola, and the others argued and strategized. These were ancient, experienced people—Jade understood they were not going to rush headlong into a fight they knew they couldn't win. They needed action, the time was urgent—yet by the time the sun had slipped down in the west and night had fallen, they still had no answers. No strategy. No idea what to do.

Some argued that they should stop talking and rush down to face Declan, but everyone ultimately rejected the idea as being merely a rushed death. Others began preparing the cloud fortress's defenses. They knew, though, that even those would not be enough. Declan was too powerful. Nobody could stop him.

Jade looked from the arguing group to the forgetting stone, back in its place on top of the little column. Starlight glinted on the black rock's smooth surface. It would be so easy to touch it, say good-bye, and forget all that had happened. Let go of this fight. Die ignorant, but without the pain of knowing that they were arguing about how best to fail.

Die.

Yes. Death was all that was left.

The voices around her rose and smacked together, a rockslide of arguments and discord. Jade stood.

"Shut up, all of you!" she shouted. "We have no idea what to do."

Mola stood and touched Jade on the shoulder. "There is only one thing for us to do," she said. "We resist him anyway."

Jade shook her head. Mola didn't know Declan like she did. Not yet. If he got the power he sought, there would be nowhere to run. No place would be safe. No person would be spared.

"If we do nothing, then death is certain," said Pola, standing at his wife's side and taking her hand.

Jade nodded. "Even if Declan destroys us, maybe we can take him down with us."

Rucksack stared at her, and Jade could see in his gaze that he already knew what she was going to say.

"We have to go down," said Jade. "All of us. We have to get me close to him. He's powerful... but his feelings for me give him conflict—and weakness. If there's a way to destroy him, I will find it." Her eyes narrowed. "And I will end him. No matter what."

Some people gasped. Some shook their heads. But mostly people nodded.

Jade's eyes burned. She had found the force attacking the Heart, and she knew she could stop him, but there was no way to do so without dying. She wanted to stop him, she needed to—the world needed her to—but she didn't want to die. Jade wanted to turn away, but she made herself stand before them and hold her gaze as steady as she could manage. She looked around the circular room, taking in the shocked and surprised faces of the people of the Heart. Her gaze passed over the forgetting stone. She looked upon Rucksack, Mola, Pola, Taras, and all the other people she had gotten to know.

Mola came over and stood next to him. "We meet him head on. No matter what."

Pola came over too, followed by Rucksack. Rucksack's face was grim, and Jade could see no light in his eyes. They hadn't looked so dark since she had first found him.

"If we must die," he said, "we can at least die defending our own and trying to do the right thing. Better to die brave than live afraid."

"Go now and prepare," said Mola.

"We leave in twenty minutes," said Pola.

She cut through the crowd and left the circular room through the western door. Rucksack started to follow her, but his grandmother touched his arm and shook her head.

Outside the citadel, Jade walked through the empty streets of the cloud fortress. This high up in the sky, it was cold, but not as cold as she would have expected. The cloud held onto the heat, Rucksack had explained, helping them stay warm.

"You can understand how they feel," said a voice.

Jade turned. Taras had followed her.

"Sure," said Jade. "They've been tucked away for so long that they never thought they would be threatened here. They thought that as long as they were apart, they would be safe." She couldn't keep the bitterness out of her voice.

"You know what it is to be apart too," said Taras, her voice soft.

"I was never safe," said Jade. "Even now. As a Jade. I knew there would be danger. I knew that being apart wasn't the same as being safe."

"But you didn't expect that the moment you left your training, you'd wind up in such an impossible situation."

"Maybe I should have told him yes," said Jade. "Declan told me that if I came back to him, he'd stop. At least while I lived, he wouldn't ruin the world. Maybe I should have accepted his offer. Gone with him. Bought us some time."

Taras's earthy brown eyes were gentle and kind. "I would've turned him down too," she said. "No one worth being with would force someone to make that sort of choice."

"How are you so kind right now?" asked Jade. "How are you not furious? At me? At this situation?"

"Aren't you furious with us?" replied Taras.

"What, because I don't think you took this seriously enough?"

"Yes."

"Then yes," said Jade. "I'm angry."

"We knew he might get through," said Taras. "It still surprised us, but we knew it was possible. We didn't think that he would be too powerful to stop."

"Slight miscalculation."

"We've never seen power like this before," said Taras. "It's another reason we talk of returning to the wider world." Sadness came into her eyes. "We've been away too long. Didn't see enough of the world's changes. Aren't in touch with what things are like now. We may live in a mountain called the Heart of the World, but we've forgotten the depth of the human heart. If we're going to help, we also have to understand what people's lives are like. What challenges they face. What glories and despairs are part of their every day."

"I don't want death and failure," said Jade. Steel came into her voice. "I want to win. I want to defeat Declan. I want to save the world. That's what I was chosen to do. I want the world safe. I don't know how to get there."

"Forget about Declan," said Taras. "If you think only of what will go wrong, then you have set your course. Right now, think only of what you want tomorrow to be like. Think of what you would want Declan's defeat to look like. Imagine it. Know it in your mind, not as if it were a possibility, but a memory.'

"And then what?"

Taras smiled. "Then do what you can to make it that way for real."

Jade tried to imagine it. Declan changing his mind, changing his heart, changing the destiny he didn't have. Realizing he was wrong. That life was pain, but that's not all it was. Jade imagined him leaving. He could build a peaceful life somewhere else. He could lay aside the power he had found, and instead learn other ways to soothe his pain and fury. She tried to see herself going to Agamuskara, standing behind the bar at the Everest Base Camp Pub and Hostel.

But all those imaginings fell to ash. Declan's fury erupted in her mind, too real to wish away.

"I can't see it," said Jade. "He's too angry. Too powerful. And we have no way to stop him."

"It will come to you," said Taras, turning to go back to the citadel. "I must get ready."

"Taras, wait," said Jade.

Taras stopped and faced Jade.

Jade took a deep breath. "Why did you help me, that day? You didn't know me. You don't know the future. Why do it?"

Taras smiled. "Because of the plea in your eyes," she replied. "When you meet someone who needs a kindness, you give it to them."

As Taras walked away, Jade went to the western edge of the cloud fortress. She told those there to go back to the citadel and said that she would watch Declan and inform them of any changes.

Jade stared down at him. Starlight glinted on the invulnerable protection that covered him. He'd become such a monster. How could she find a kindness for him now?

Standing at the edge in the middle of the deep night, Jade could see only the vast darkness over the world. She turned and looked south, toward India, toward Agamuskara. She wondered if she would ever get there.

"Now I'm here instead," said Jade. "Where nothing makes sense. Where I don't know what I'm doing. Where I'm destined to fail, when I thought I my path was to make everything right. Now we're all about to die. And it's all because dumping my boyfriend made him so crazy he wants to destroy the world."

Standing high above the world, Jade had never felt so low in her life.

Then, behind her, there was a glow.

26

RETURN

This time the glow wasn't the soft, subtle yet world-changing arrival of dawn. No light was breaking over the eastern mountains yet.

Instead, The Management had appeared.

They floated in the darkness. The figure in blue and gold was to Jade's left. The figure in brown and black was to Jade's right. Between them floated the figure in gold and silver.

Her gaze hard, Jade stared at them. She wondered what would happen if she punched them.

"You lot," she said, her voice low with a hint of a growl. "I don't suppose you've come to do something useful? If not, you can bugger off back to whatever office you stay in when you're not out here screwing with people."

"It's not our place to do more, Jade Agamuskara Bluegold," said The Management. Their eerie three-as-one voice sounded dull on the cloud.

Jade's eyes narrowed. "That's not what I was going to say."

"But it's what you mean."

They had her there.

"The people of the world are not ours to keep as pets," said

The Management. "We are the custodians of existence. We do not own life. We do not control life. We only try to help."

"Then who's in charge? Who owns life? Who controls it?"

The way The Management tilted their hooded heads, it was as if she had surprised them.

"You mean you don't know?" The Management shifted forward. "All this time? All you've learned? And you don't know?"

"I'm not out here in the middle of the night, right before I die, to ask rhetorical questions," said Jade. "Who's in charge of you?"

"The same beings who have always been in charge," said The Management. "You. Life is in charge of life. Life controls life. We are The Management. We work for you, and for all other life in this world."

"You're like guardrails," said Jade. "There's a road, but sometimes people still veer off and crash through."

"As an analogy, it will suffice." The Management paused, as if deciding how much more to say. "We never make the decisions, Jade. We sense what life wants and try to encourage things to go that way. We nudge. We don't shove."

"Seems like you gave me a big push," said Jade. "Followed by a kick up the arse."

"We help as we can. And you are not a regular person," replied The Management. "People have to decide for themselves whether they want this world to continue and how life will be. All that matters in the world is that we care enough about living in it to do better things."

"And if we don't?" Jade pointed down, toward the still figure below. "What about when someone like Declan happens?" The anger came out now. "Where is your help and nudging then, huh? All these years he's been wandering, fueled by fury and agony, and what have you done to help him?"

"We can only help those who want help," said The Management. "For all his pain and rage, he did not want help. He is beyond our influence. He has no destiny. He does not even truly choose. He is at the mercy of his pain. In the midst of all that pain, we found one little thread that we could use. He kept calling out for you. He always had a wish to see you again."

"Well, he got it," said Jade. "Fat bloody lot of good it did too. I made him all the more determined to destroy the world."

"You are not responsible for what happened in Hong Kong."

"Declan says I am." She shook her head. "In some ways, he's right. I chose to leave. Look what happened as a result. All that blood. One of our own, Jake Hongkong, gone." She leaned forward, all but spitting at them. "You should have told me the truth. That I was coming here to face my old boyfriend. You should have told me what had happened to him."

"We gave you only what you needed to get going," said The Management. "For the rest, we trusted you. We trusted your ability to face the challenges that would confront you, and to learn from them. Above all, Jade Agamuskara Bluegold, we trusted your heart. And we still believe we were right. You have met challenge after challenge. You have learned and accepted. You found and befriended Rucksack. You learned to fly. You braved the mountains and their challenges to reach the Heart of the World—the first in millennia to do so. Now you're standing on a cloud, something a few days ago you didn't even know was possible. You have done so much, Jade. Now we ask for only one more thing."

"After all this, what could you ask for, that I could do?"

"We ask for your forgiveness."

"You want me... to forgive you? For this little stunt you've pulled with your rookie?"

"Yes. And for much else," said The Management. "Declan is our fault, not yours. We know that we can seem cruel or heartless. We know that you see us as manipulative. It's understandable. But we serve life, Jade. Hong Kong and what happened since with Declan was beyond our control and influence. We could not stop these things. We are not all-powerful, Jade. We do what we can for the life we serve."

Jade took a step toward The Management. "Did you make Declan the way he is now?"

"No," replied The Management. "He did. We did not make him go to the pub. We did not make him lose his destiny. He chose those things."

"But afterward?"

"Even afterward, this darkness did not have to consume him," said The Management. "All beings have darkness. All life must decide how much or how little light to have too. Declan likes his darkness. He likes his rage and his agony. They fuel him. Drive him. And consume him. He hates them too, but he no longer sees any other choices. Instead of facing his agony and wrongdoing, he let it fester and mutate. Now hatred fills him, and the need to control and dominate is the only way he sees to stop his pain. This is not our fault. It is not your fault. This is the destiny that Declan made for himself: a tyrannical need to dominate and destroy."

For long quiet minutes, Jade stared at them. She felt her own struggle between the light and darkness inside. But she saw where her balance could lie.

"I forgive you," she whispered. She looked up at them, and her voice found more strength and confidence. "I forgive you, as I forgive myself. But that doesn't mean I want to work with you. If I survive this, I shouldn't be a Jade after all. Maybe I was wrong and you were too. I don't know how you can trust me after this, and I don't see how the hells I can trust you."

"When this is all over," said The Management, "if you survive and want to leave the Jakes and Jades, we will honor your wish."

"You will? That simple?"

"Yes. We will change your memory so that you do not remember any of your time as a Jade, or any of this. You will live a long, happy life."

Jade said nothing. She had thought that being a Jade was what she wanted. The reality, though, of what The Management had done...

"Okay then," she said at last. "You want my help? Then tell me the whole truth, not the damn little crumbs you think I deserve to get me going. Tell me the truth and I accept."

"Of course, Jade," said The Management. "You're right. We're sorry."

"What should I do now?" asked Jade

"Giving outright advice isn't our job," said The Management. "Life must figure out its course. We're here to help."

"Right now, any help would be a big help," replied Jade.

"As you wish," said The Management. "If you want to prevail over Declan, you must hold the center yet also lose it."

"Hold the center yet also lose it?" asked Jade. "What the hell does that mean?"

"All we know is that is what life says you should know," said The Management. "The rest, we're afraid, is up to you."

They began to fade, the darkness becoming more visible through their translucent forms.

"Wait!" said Jade. "Come on, there has to be more. Please, tell me!"

But The Management was gone.

Jade looked down. Declan was gone too. Jade glanced left and right, up and down. How could he have slipped away? Had he managed to get inside after all? Jade's heart pounded, and her hands clenched into fists. The air of the cloud fortress suddenly seemed too thin—

From the base of the Heart of the World, the essence of a furious scream managed to make it all the way to Jade's ears. She stopped. And grinned.

Declan stepped back into view; he must have been surveying the damage to his precious handiwork. He stared hard at the cloud fortress, and Jade figured he was beginning to suspect something. Yet he looked away, then raised his hands. Blasts of red and orange energy flew from him, and once again Declan began trying to clear his way into the Heart of the World.

Jade's eyes narrowed. "One way or another," she said, "I'm going to stop you. No matter what it takes."

Jade rushed back to the citadel. "Declan's on the move," she said. "Time's up."

Rucksack came over and touched her shoulder with his left hand. With his right, he handed her a short, curved knife, in a simple black scabbard. "May you find a way," he said.

Jade stared at her friend, at everyone around them. She nodded. "May we all."

"You understand the difference now," said Rucksack. "Between despair and hope."

"Yes," said Jade, as she took the knife. "Just because I feel despair doesn't mean I have to let it rule me. I despair that we may fail. Likely will fail. But I'll hold my head high, because there's just the one slight sliver of hope that we might get through this and Declan might fall."

Rucksack smiled and he gave her shoulder a squeeze. "If we make it out o' this, Jade Bluegold, I hope that we have many years o' friendship to look forward to."

Jade clapped her opposite hand to his shoulder. "Aye, my friend," she replied. "Me too. But since we likely won't, I hope you know how much I've appreciated the friendship we've had."

Rucksack nodded. "Same here, my friend."

Mola came over. "Are you ready?"

With a nod, Jade tucked the knife at the small of her back and joined Rucksack, Mola, Pola, Taras, and the other people of the Heart of the World. They stood in a circle around the southern end of the room.

The first rays of the new day's sunlight began to shine into the room. Light glinted off the stone and the pillar and the dark walls.

And Jade smiled.

"What is it?" asked Rucksack.

"We don't need to despair at all," said Jade.

"We've got the light in our hearts," said Rucksack. "Joy and love, despite all else. Hopefully those things can survive, even if we don't."

"There's that," said Jade. She grinned and shook her head. "And there's one other thing."

Afraid yet resolute, Jade told them her plan.

When she finished, no one said anything. Some looked astounded. Some looked troubled. But if anyone objected, they didn't say anything—and after all, it was the only plan they had.

In silence, every person nodded their agreement.

Mola, Pola, and Rucksack left for a few minutes. To get the show in motion, as Rucksack put it.

When they returned to the circle, everyone stared at the cloud floor, trying to feel resolute. No one felt ready to return to the mountain, but they were ready to return, because they had to be.

Jade stood before the center of the floor, and in her mind asked it to open.

Before them, the cloud floor faded away. A long, vertical, cylindrical passage through the cloud fortress appeared. It opened at the bottom over the jagged hole in the top of the Heart of the World. Below them the rising sun began to brighten the mountain, but the broken, jagged summit remained in darkness.

Lightness in Jade's heart filled her body, mind, and soul. She smiled at the others and said, "Don't be afraid. We're going to win."

Then she jumped—and said uncertainly, under her breath, "If this actually works."

27

HUNT

Around Jade the cloud darkened, and the true power of the cloud fortress came to life.

The silvery gray faded to deep dark grays and whirling blacks. Thunder rumbled throughout the mass of cloud. A charge in the air lifted Jade's hair off her head.

As she and the others descended through the cloud, a chill crept through Jade. Below them, the bottom opening came closer. Then they emerged, into the clear gap between the cloud and the mountain.

Looking down, she was certain she had seen Declan, near the base of the mountain, still trying to blast his way back inside. She smiled and wondered what he was thinking now.

Jade looked up. The cloud fortress had turned black, a thunderhead the size of a mountain that made Everest look like a hill. Beneath the cloud fortress's outer layer, silver and gold flashes bloomed and faded. The buzzing air tasted metallic.

The air was also so cold and thin, Jade could hardly breathe, and her skin went numb. Winds smacked at Jade and the others. Its rush filled her ears, as if they had dropped into a tornado. Jade veered back and forth, trying not to collide with anyone.

"Focus," said Rucksack. "You can adjust how you fly to work with the wind."

Jade followed his movements. Though the wind still beat at her, she stayed on course toward the jagged opening at the top of the Heart of the World.

The cloud fortress unleashed its power.

Hail the size of boulders rained down like bombs around the mountain's base. Spikes of silver and gold lightning stabbed the mountain and the surrounding plain. Jade hoped one of them would spear Declan like a fish. Then at least this would all be over—and she wouldn't have to go through with the plan after all.

She had flown too low now to see Declan, and could only hope. They wouldn't know Declan's fate until they faced him inside. Or if they emerged outside and found his charred ruins smoking beyond the mountain walls.

They dropped past the jagged summit and entered the Heart of the World. Immediately the wind was gone, and silence filled Jade. So did warmth. The inside of the mountain radiated, as if they were in the tropics instead of the Tibetan Himalayas. Jade looked around. The sun had not risen high enough to pour light into the mountain. They were relying on darkness—and the cloud fortress's artillery show—to help them pass into the mountain unseen. If Declan had escaped the hail and lightning, he was likely making his way through to the center.

"Is the warmth anything you did?" Jade asked Mola.

"No," she replied. "The mountain is a volcano. The Heart of the World is a beautiful place, but it can be harsh too. There can be love and peace here, but there can also be destruction."

"Hundreds of millions of years ago," said Pola, "volcanic eruptions eradicated almost all life on the planet. That all began here. This volcano erupted, and it set off a chain reaction of other eruptions."

"That's what Declan's come to understand," said Jade. "That's what he wants to do again, except he means to make sure that no life remains this time."

Despite what she had learned, Jade found a way to keep her heart light. She focused on their plan, on all the hope she was putting into it. Reaching back, Jade checked that the knife was still tucked into her waistband, at the small of her back. In front of her, Taras turned and gave her a small smile, though she was so covered in shadow that Jade nearly missed it. Jade smiled back, hoping Taras saw. Glancing back up toward the summit, Jade saw the morning sunlight glow on the jagged mountaintop. making it look like a crown.

Jade's feet touched down without a sound. She jumped—and almost squealed. The ground was hot, and seemed to be getting hotter.

Rucksack squatted and touched the ground. "The Heart is responding to Declan," he said. "It knows the darkness that has come here."

They looked around—and stopped. In the distance, shadows were moving toward them.

Jade felt her body tense, and she could feel a similar anticipation in the others. Was Declan here? Had he conjured some strange power?

Then faces appeared—and relief flooded Jade.

The people who had left the cloud fortress earlier appeared. They came over. They reported that all was in readiness, but they had seen no sign of Declan.

Around them all, sun shone through the windows in the underside of the mountain slope. The Heart of the World began to glow. Around Jade, animals slept in large pens. Narrow lanes separated fields of barley. Plants grew inside large clear structures, except for one plant. At the center of the vast space inside the mountain, a gnarled cherry tree grew.

At the heart of such a force of destruction, the people had created a place of life and peace.

"I can see why it's hard to leave," said Jade softly. "You've made this place a paradise."

Mola smiled. "It took many years," she said. "But years we had, along with no little skill and perseverance. We only wanted to have enough, so that we could live together in peace. Then we could prepare for when it was time to return to the world again."

"I wish I could have seen more of what you've done here," said Jade.

Pola nodded, his eyes glinting dimly with resigned sadness. "As do I, child."

Mola and Pola led them down a path toward where the inside slope of the mountain met the ground at a steep angle. A tall oval entrance had been cut into the rock. "Through here is where we must go," said Mola. "Deep inside the mountain lies a fault that goes deep, deep into the earth.

"It is where the force from long ago rose up," said Pola. "And it is what Declan will use now."

"We should be getting there before him though," said Rucksack. "Let's get down there and set up. We can keep surprise on our side and end this."

Rucksack, Mola, and Pola led the group. At the far end, Jade and Taras kept an eye out for Declan.

"Remember that Declan doesn't know we're around. He'll think he's alone here," said Jade. She touched the handle of the knife at her back. "We need to surprise him. Hold him off as long as you can, and I'll do the rest. No matter what."

The passage twisted and turned for miles. Always it angled downward, deeper into the earth. With every curve and bend, Jade sensed that they were also angling more toward the center of the mountain.

Finally, they emerged into a wide tall chamber, roughly circular. The group spread out in a crescent. At the center, a glowing red mass, like a steeple or spire, rose so high that it almost touched the ceiling. The mass popped and rumbled, a dull, constant roar. Jade stared toward the top. The hot dry air made Jade's skin feel leathery. She was certain that if she stood on top of the spire and could see through the mountain, she would see the Heart's jagged summit. Jade made to go to the front, to stand with Rucksack, Mola, and Pola, but Taras held her back.

"What are you doing?" asked Jade.

"Problem," said Taras.

Before them, a shadow stood in front of the red mass.

"So much for time," said Jade.

"Stay out here," said Taras, tucking Jade outside the entrance to the chamber, behind the rock.

"But the plan." Jade reached for the knife at the small of her back.

Taras shrugged. "No more plan. Stay here."

As if he had a crown on his head and a scepter up his arse, Declan turned to face them. "I was starting to think there was no one here. Thought you had all died, tucked away in here all these eons."

"We're here now," said Rucksack, stepping forward, away from the others.

Declan smiled. "You were up on that strange cloud, weren't you? I can only guess that you've managed something magical and powerful. After you're dead, I'll find my way there, learn your secrets, and put all that you made to my own uses."

Jade's eyes widened. She could imagine it now—the cloud fortress flying to city after city and decimating all life and resistance with storms of hail and lightning.

Rucksack took a step back so that he was sideways to Declan.

Declan snorted. "Please," he said. "I can fight all of you and win. Easily."

"We have not come to fight," said Rucksack. "We want to talk."

"No need," said Declan. "You already know how close I am. The power here knows me. It wants me. Power doesn't want to rest. Power wants to be used. Soon, I'll be more powerful than you could imagine. It's a rather nice feeling. Like waking up on your birthday and knowing there'll be a big party later."

"Nothing will stand against you," said Rucksack. "No force or person or institution or anything."

"Some will try, I'm sure," said Declan. "As some will try to resist the devastation that will fall from the sky and turn the air to poison."

Declan scanned the people around him. "Where's Jade?"

"Gone," said Rucksack. "Despair overcame her. Despair at what you became. She left."

"Leaving you to try to persuade me to stop?" Declan laughed.

"I'm sorry for what happened to you," said Rucksack. "And for what has happened since. For my part, I offer my help. Together, I'll work with you. There are others paths than these. There are other ways to face the pain you feel—and to stop letting it rule you. You seek to rule because you feel out o' control. I get that. Your pain rules you. Your rage rules you. You don't want that. I can feel it in you. You want to rule you." Rucksack held out his hand. "I'll help."

Declan stared at the hand, then he chuckled and shook his head. "You have no way to help me."

"Think you and I are so different, do you?" said Rucksack. "I lost my destiny too, Declan. I failed to prevent The Blast. I was right there when it happened. I didn't die, but my destiny did. I know what you know. I feel what you feel. As far as I know, you and I are the only people in the world like this: unmoored and adrift. I am lost and alone in this world. I am weak and scared. My every moment is pain, and if you think I don't know rage and fury, think again. I know them in myself, and I feel them for myself. For my failure. I feel them every day."

"But you do not use them."

"Oh, but I do. The anger is there. The pain is there." Rucksack held up his gloved left hand, held in a fist so tight his arm trembled. "But it's not allowed to rule." He opened his hand. "Life is a constant question of yes or no, life or death, love or fear. How we answer is what decides our every moment and destiny. I use my anger. I transform it into hope. I turn pain into doing, helping, improving. You can too. If we work together."

"There is only suffering," said Declan.

"There is suffering," replied Rucksack. "But there's also not letting it win. There's meeting it with doing, caring, loving, trying. The cure for suffering is not to cause death and cessation, but to counter it with love and joy. Death merely ends. But love is something else, and it grows more than suffering. You want to beat suffering. That's the better way."

"I'm doing it one better," said Declan. "I'm ending the game."

Behind Declan, the red mass flared upward again. The room rumbled and shook, and Jade broke out in a sweat. It hurt to breathe the hot air.

"You're a fool, Faddah Rucksack," said Declan. "Suffering long ago outpaced love. Why do you think all these people shut themselves up in a mountain? They know the world is lost." He shrugged. "It needs to find the end. I'm the guide who is going to do just that. The end starts now."

Some of the red glow began to come together in long, skinny shapes, like tentacles. They wound their way down from the top of the mass to Declan's head and back. He began to glow too, filling with the power of the life-consuming fire.

Rucksack ran forward. So did Mola, Pola, and the people of the Heart. Taras ran forward too. They all ran, yelling, ready to do all they could—

A red-and-black wave shot through the room. Rucksack, Mola, Pola, Taras, and all the other people of the Heart fell to the ground.

"No!" yelled Jade. She stepped out from behind the rock and entered the chamber.

Declan smiled at her. "I had a feeling Rucksack was lying

about you," he said. "Don't worry. I didn't kill them. Yet. In fact, now that I can feel the fire, I have a better idea. Killing them will be so easy, and there is so much life to wipe out. It will be hard to do it by myself. But with the power of the fire, I don't have to do it alone. When my eyes turn red and black, I will have the power of the fire. Then, I can take over these people's destinies. Their decisions, their very wills and actions and selves, will all be mine." Declan grinned like a scythe. Jade hoped the corners of his mouth would poke his eyes out.

"You still won't have your own destiny," said Jade.

Declan shrugged. "Who cares? I'll have theirs instead."

Behind Declan, the red mass glowed brighter. Plumes of magma shot into the air, scorching the ceiling—and starting to melt it. Black drops rained to the floor.

Jade feared her lungs would catch fire.

"I will control them," said Declan. "They'll be my little puppets, on my strings. Even better? They'll know everything that is happening to them. Every horror that I make them commit. But they won't be able to do anything about it." He glared at Rucksack. "I can't wait to see what horrors I will make him do, and know that he is helpless."

Declan's eyes began to glow a soft yet fiery red.

28

BLAST

The magma behind Declan grew taller now. When it touched the surrounding walls, they began to shudder and melt. The chamber rumbled and shook.

Beneath Jade, the fire pressed to break free and set loose its horrible blast upon the world. The people around her would be Declan's slaves. The world would burn. The fire of life would go out, extinguished by the molten flame and the murdering ash of death.

For a moment, Jade closed her eyes. "Hold the center yet also lose it," she whispered. "Hold the center yet also lose it."

She had tried to hold the center. Tried to hold Declan's heart. Tried to devote her full self to being a Jade. Tried to be the hero and the champion that this quest had needed. There was nothing left now. Only this moment, this last moment before the fire. Opening her eyes, Jade understood.

Stepping closer, Jade reached behind her. She pulled out the knife, scabbard and all, from her waistband, and held it out in front of her.

Declan chuckled. "You came to kill me, then?"

A tear came down Jade's cheek, and with a whisper the tear was gone in the growing heat that filled the chamber.

Jade nodded. She let the other tears come and have their brief moment in the sad dying world.

"But I was wrong," she said, and she opened her hand. The scabbarded knife clattered on the stony floor. "I was wrong about everything," she said. "But especially about you. I'm sorry."

Declan's eyes glowed red. Around them, hissing in the heat, she could see the tracks of tears. The price of power was burning.

Jade came close to him, and she touched his cheek. She could feel it now. Where his past had been, a dark void had invaded and taken over. Before him, where others might find destiny, possibility, potential, there was only more void. Declan's life had become a single point, as if he had not existed, had no more past, and also had no future before him. Yet, in his eyes, she could see that he knew what had happened, and what he had lost. The pain of that loss, the pain of being trapped, burned in him far more painfully than any fire of the world ever could. As Jade looked at him, pity filled her.

"You don't need to burn," she said. "You lost what you knew. But you didn't lose everything. You have choice. Choice is all the power, all the destiny you'll ever need. It's a matter of what you choose."

Declan shook his head. "I have only this now."

"You have pain. I feel it in you. The loneliness. The fear of being weak." Jade stroked his cheek with one hand. She saw the plea in his eyes—and thought of the one kindness she could give.

With her other hand she slowly, quietly unbuttoned the cargo pocket on her left leg. "You feel completely disconnected from the world. You believe you are powerless to do anything, change anything, be anything, strive for anything."

Declan nodded. More tears came down now, and not all hissed away. He touched a hand to her cheek. The red glow in his eyes faded, until only blue shone again.

Jade nodded. She leaned forward and rested his forehead against hers. "It doesn't have to be this way. You can turn away from this," she said. "I feel your wish to be free of your pain and be yourself again. I feel the longing in you."

"Is that what you also feel?"

"For us?" said Jade. "I'm sorry, Declan, but no. You don't need to look back at what we had. You can look ahead."

"Ever since that day in Hong Kong, I've looked ahead," said Declan. "All I see is darkness. That's the destiny I'm choosing to fulfill. It's all I've got."

"I forgive you," said Jade. "For Hong Kong. For this. I cannot take away your pain, but you can change what it means to you."

Declan pulled back from her. The red glow in his eyes deepened again.

"But Declan is dead," he said. "That's a name, a self, that I'm leaving behind. There is no destiny. There is no choice. There is only power, and pain, and the need to use power to end the pain forever. There is only control and being controlled. Declan is dead," he said again. He smiled. "I am Tiran now."

He knocked away Jade's hand and shoved her backward, across the chamber. She smacked hard against the far wall and fell to the floor.

"The power is ready for me now," he said, "and I am ready for the power."

A hint of black shone in his eyes. Behind him, the magma rose through the shattered ceiling. It began its rise to the unsuspecting world beyond.

"I know," said Jade. "You have to hold the center, yet also lose it. I'm ready too." She shook her head and stood. "Declan?"

"That name is no more—"

"I wish you had made a better choice," she said.

Doubt surged in her. What would happen? Was she doing the right thing? Would any of them survive? Would the world?

Declan raised his hands toward Jade. She could feel the fire now. Heat singed her eyebrows. Declan's hands glowed orange, then red, streaked with black.

One more tear came down Jade's own cheek. In the moment before the heat burned it away, Jade wondered what would happen after. Her mind tried to hold on to the friends she had made, and all she had learned and come to understand. But beyond all that, she understood that it didn't matter now. She had held on to the center as long as she could. Now it was time to lose it.

Fire and chill rose up in Jade. A tear hung on her cheek, yet she could feel the steel inside her soul. All that mattered was what had to be done, no matter what else. Despite all that care and fear, all that heaviness, Jade found a lightness in her heart.

Out of the corner of her eye, she saw Rucksack leap up. As he ran toward Declan, a roar like a tiger's filled the chamber.

Rucksack grabbed Declan's hands and pulled them away. "Now!" shouted Rucksack.

"With you hanging on?" said Jade. "You know what will happen."

"Yes, damn it," said Rucksack. "Do it now!"

"I'm sorry."

Rucksack shook his head. "Better sorry than dead."

No matter how hard Declan struggled, Rucksack held on. The lightness in her heart driving her, Jade flew across the chamber. As she landed before Declan, she reached into her left cargo pocket and drew out the forgetting stone, which she had pulled from its pedestal in the final minutes before they had all left the citadel.

Fire erupted from Declan, ringing his entire body and threatening to burn them all.

Jade ignored the biting flames. She ignored the pain inside too. She wanted to hold on to the memories, the friendships, and all she had learned. To Declan. To Rucksack. To knowing how to fly. To the Heart of the World. To Taras, Mola, Pola, all the people and experiences she was about to lose.

Better to forget everything about this place, though, than for Declan to win. Holding Declan's neck, Jade slammed the forgetting stone against his forehead.

"Good-bye," said Jade, to her recent memories, to everything the stone would make her forget.

White light filled the chamber.

Then darkness.

29

ARRIVAL

Jade couldn't remember what had happened in the dream, but she remembered how she felt.

She had been so unsettled and afraid, then conflicted and filled with despair. But there had been a brightness there too, a gleam in the dark. Hope and friendship. Surprise and joy. A feeling of sheer lightness that had made her feel so wonderful it was as if she were flying.

Sitting up on her train berth, Jade shook off the night's rest. Out the train window, she watched the western side of the world as the train rode south toward Agamuskara. For a train ride, she had slept incredibly well, as if she had been asleep for days, not hours.

Raising her arms and stretching, Jade glanced around. Other people were rising as well, waking with the first light of morning. Soft murmurs susurrated around the train.

Jade nodded good morning to two men in the berths across from her. They looked familiar, yet she could have sworn there were different people there yesterday.

The boy was gone. To be on the safe side, Jade checked her pockets, her daypack, and her rucksack. Everything was right where it should be. Time passed. She thought the boy might have gone to the toilet. Perhaps he was elsewhere on the train, steeling himself for arrival in Agamuskara. She hoped he hadn't lost his nerve and gotten off at an earlier stop.

When the conductor passed by, Jade motioned to him. "The boy sitting with me, who I bought a ticket for," she said. "Is he still on board?"

The conductor shrugged and moved on. Jade decided not to worry about it. Instead she hoped.

Someday the boy would come see her at the pub. She could stand him a drink while listening to stories of his life since the day they had met on the train.

The countryside began to give way to the outskirts of Agamuskara. Jade thought of pictures she'd seen, of the city center with its brilliant white stone buildings. Even out here, white stone gleamed in the morning sunshine. The little huts were small, but they shone with no less brilliance.

Children ran alongside the train. Women in bright, colorful saris walked while carrying bundles of food. With every clack of the train's wheels over the tracks, the buildings became bigger, more numerous, more tightly packed together. Jade pulled together her things. She nipped to the toilet cubicle to make sure she was ready for the day.

This was it.

Agamuskara.

Her first day as a Jade. Jade Agamuskara Bluegold.

Soon the train slowed and came to a stop outside the main station. Jade hoisted her large rucksack onto her back, then swung her small daypack over her chest. The two men in the berth opposite hers had already left the train. Jade joined the press of people making their way to the platform.

The air's wet heat met her first, followed by the sun's ever-hotter glow. Millions of voices and noises surged throughout the city. The air all but shimmered with an energy and vibrancy that Jade hadn't felt since Hong Kong.

Even here, on the platform, she could smell the city. Charcoal fires smoked. Spices from a thousand food stalls and restaurants wafted through the air. Cow dung added its soft sharp surprise to every inhale. The cow responsible, pale white and skinny, wove its way through the crowded platform. Jade chuckled as she made her way to the street.

"What do you think of our city?" said a man leaning against a black-and-yellow taxi. His words had a bubbly quality to them, as if he were speaking with a dialect, yet also having a joke on her. Another man was sitting in the taxi's driver seat.

Jade grinned. "I love it here already."

"Tourist?" asked the man behind the wheel. He bobbed his head. Both men looked so familiar. Faces from some other strange corner of the world. Yet remembering them was past the edge of Jade's memory. Oh well.

Jade reminded herself that in the years to come, she would see so many faces new and familiar, or seemingly familiar yet new all the same. These two were the beginning. They had to be brothers, though.

"Not a tourist," said Jade. "New local. I'm here for a job."

"Ah!" The man leaning against the taxi pushed off and stood straight. "My brother knows a shopkeeper who needs a good assistant—"

"Sorry, lads," said Jade. "I've already got a job. I'm the new bartender at the Everest Base Camp Pub and Hostel."

The man opened the taxi's back door. "Our favorite pub!"

"It's an honor to take you there," said the man behind the wheel. "No charge."

"That's most kind," said Jade as she shrugged off her two packs. She winked. "I'm sure there could be a free pint with your name on it some night."

"We like you already," said the first man, as he put Jade's rucksack in the trunk. "Just what the Everest needed."

He held open the rear left door for Jade as she got in and set her daypack next to her. He closed the door and got in front next to his brother. Then they were underway.

Jade watched the city as they drove. She chatted with the brothers about Agamuskara—where to go, who to know, what to do. They rode over the river, also named Agamuskara. To the west, moving north, Jade spotted a large cloud. It was the size of a mountain, but it was even bigger than Everest, the tallest mountain in the world. She'd never seen anything like it, yet like the brothers' faces, something about it tugged at the edges of her memory.

"Hey," said Jade to the brothers.

"Yes?" said the driver.

"Why were the river and city both named 'smiling fire?'"

The brothers bobbed their heads. "No one knows," said the other. "Maybe you'll find out someday."

Before Jade knew it, they had pulled up in front of the Everest Base Camp Pub and Hostel. It was the finest of its kind in the city and, many said, in all India.

Jade grinned and got out of the taxi. Backpacks on, she went up to the door as the brothers drove away. She paused though. For a moment she looked from the top of the building to the base, and down the full length of the gleaming white walls. She smiled.

It was time.

Come what may, she knew that she could handle being a Jade and all the difficult decisions she would have to make.

Inside, her future waited. Jade opened the door.

PART IV

30

SPARK

The sun began to rise over Chomolungma. On the mountain's summit two figures waited in deep thought and concentration. As the darkness began to break, they tried to divert the ferocious gales around them. The wind kept trying to blow them off the summit of what other people thought to be the world's tallest mountain.

The people could hold off the wind, but there was no way to completely block out the cold. The chill bit into the bones and slowed the blood, and the thin air still burned their lungs and fogged their minds. The sooner they could leave, the better, but first they had to complete their task. The time was now. No matter the wind or cold, there would be no leaving until the spark was lit.

Before them, three figures began to appear, at first translucent, then solidifying. Soon, the three hooded figures of The Management floated above the ice and snow of the summit. The figure in gold and silver was in the middle, flanked by the figure in blue and gold and the figure in brown and black.

"We meet again," said Mola.

"And for the same purpose," replied The Management. "May it go better this time."

"What happened the day of The Blast was not our doing or yours," said Pola.

"That spark became something we could not expect or control," said The Management. "Are you certain of the destiny you hope for this one?"

"We can only create the spark when someone performs an act of love and bravery beyond compare," said Mola.

"You know as well as we do that such a thing has happened," said Pola.

"Not without unforeseen consequences," said The Management.

Mola shrugged. "What does?"

"We know what happened to Jade," said The Management. "After you woke, you discovered she had lost her memory of all that had happened—the train ride, the trek, Rucksack, the Heart of the World, Declan."

"Do you think she knew what would happen?" said Mola.

"For the sake of stopping Declan, we think it was a risk she was willing to take," said The Management. "What became of the others?"

"We dropped Rucksack and Declan far away, in different corners of the world," said Pola. "Rucksack forgot flying, and has decided not to try again. He also has forgotten Jade, the cloud fortress"—he sighed—"and us."

He paused a moment, then continued, trying to keep his voice steady. "Declan has forgotten his power, along with anything he knew or suspected about the Heart of the World. We're safe. For now."

The Management stared at them. "You are uncertain."

"Declan has not lost his hunger for power and dominion," said Mola. "He has forgotten, but what is forgotten may one day be remembered."

"You should not have freed him," said The Management.

"In chains, he would be a certain enemy," said Pola. "Freed... Jade has a knack for giving people second chances. Our hope is that she has given him an opportunity to change."

"What he does with that," said Mola, "the destiny he chooses... that is up to him."

The Management floated so that now Mola and Pola interspersed them and formed a circle. They stared at the space in the middle. "Will it be for Rucksack or for Jade?"

"It may be for neither. It could be for someone we have yet to meet," said Mola. "None will know until the time."

The Management nodded, and they all began.

Long hours passed. The sun traveled over the mountain. Clouds gathered. Snow and ice lashed them. The wind blew harder than ever, as if wanting to sheer the very top off the mountain. Lightning pounded the rock around the five figures. Through it all they paid no mind. They kept their heads bowed and their eyes closed. Speaking softly, they raised their arms toward the center of the circle they had created.

The elements coming together—this was part of it, after all. Over time, the snow became rain. The rain narrowed, becoming a stream that poured into the middle of the circle, as did the snow and ice. Then the air cleared. Moments later the wind began to swirl, forming a tornado that plunged into the center of the circle and was gone. The gray clouds above them darkened, blackening to a void like outer space. Brighter than the sun, lightning forked down, in brilliant silvers and golds. Within the circle, thunder cracked and boomed.

The clouds broke and vanished. All was silent.

Above the five figures, an orb like the noonday sun glowed golden, then flashed silver, then black.

Then it vanished.

The little sun returned a moment later, as if it had never left the top of its arc in the sky. In the middle of the circle, the five figures lowered their arms.

Before them, flashing gold, silver, and black, a little spark floated.

The spark rose up a little ways above their heads. There it would remain, high enough to be ignored by any who came to the summit. Yet, when the time was right, the right person would harvest the star that would grow from the little spark.

"We hope you're right about this one," said The Management. "The world may not survive another Blast."

Mola and Pola had no reply. Without another word, The Management faded, leaving behind only their unease and uncertainty. Mola and Pola reached for each other's hands. For a while, the cold and wind forgotten, they watched the little star.

"Maybe we should have told Rucksack the truth about The Blast," said Mola. "Were we wrong not to have told him everything that happened that day?"

"Don't doubt yourself," said Pola. "I still agree with you. He can only learn the truth for himself, in his own time and in his own way. When he does, all we can do is hope that it is the right time, and that he will understand."

"But Jade," said Mola. "She deserved to know more. We could have told her everything."

"I wish we could have too." Sadness and regret muted his voice and made it crack.

"She made an impossible choice," said Mola.

"That's why we're still here," said Pola.

Soon the cloud fortress came overhead. With a nod and still holding hands, Mola and Pola lifted off from the cold summit and flew to their floating home. Looking down, if they stared at an exact angle, they could make out the glint of the spark they had created. Already it was bigger, growing light and darkness, growing a choice of life or death, yes or no.

But what it would ultimately become, they could not know. They could only hope.

The cloud fortress floated away, back toward the Heart of the World. Mola and Pola watched the spark and the mountain summit fade from sight. Then they looked ahead. Toward the home they had known. Toward the world beyond, that they hoped they would come to know again.

If the world survived.

THE...
End? Nope!
More adventures await in the acclaimed Rucksack Universe.
Start your next journey at...
rucksackuniverse.com

THANK YOU FOR READING

Please **tell people** about this story and **review it at your favorite online bookstore or social network**.

Reviews are the best way readers discover great new books, and I would truly appreciate it. Even a couple of sentences is a big help.

BECOME A WANDERER

Early access to new stories... and much more
Back Anthony's fiction and non-fiction on Patreon

This story is made possible in part by my Wanderers, my patrons on Patreon. In return for backing my work each month, Wanderers can get special rewards, exclusive access to me, e-books, signed books, early access to new stories, and more. Learn more and become a patron today:

patreon.com/anthonystclair

Free ebook bundle!
3 short stories + 1 novel

When you join Anthony's free Reader Club via email, you'll get a free book bundle, hear about new stories, events, news, and more!

rucksackuniverse.com/wanderbundle

ALSO BY ANTHONY ST. CLAIR

Tap the title to learn more and buy from your favorite bookstore.

Rucksack Universe Box Set #1: Includes Wander, The Martini of Destiny, Home Sweet Road, Forever the Road, and The Lotus and the Barley

books2read.com/boxset01

Wander

rucksackuniverse.com/wander

The Martini of Destiny

rucksackuniverse.com/martini

Cloud Fortress

rucksackuniverse.com/cloudfortress

Home Sweet Road

rucksackuniverse.com/homesweetroad

Forever the Road

rucksackuniverse.com/forevertheroad

The Lotus and the Barley

rucksackuniverse.com/lotus

Short fiction

rucksackuniverse.com/stories

News, special features, and more

rucksackuniverse.com

ACKNOWLEDGMENTS

Rucksack Universe stories are made possible in part by the ongoing support of my Wanderers, my patrons on Patreon. Special thanks to patron Sean Keener. Patrons can get special rewards, exclusive access to me, early access to new stories, free books, and more. You can be a patron too. Learn more and become a patron today:

patreon.com/anthonystclair

Thank you to Bonnie Donaghy for cover design, and to Scott Alexander Jones for the spot-on copy editing, story advice, and proofreading. Any mistakes—especially when it comes to languages and cultures—are mine.

Above all, my thanks to my family. Connor and Aster, you inspire every story I write. Jodie, with you I am the man I'd always hoped to be.

ISBN, Trade Paperback Edition: 978-1-940119-22-9

ISBN, ePub Edition: 978-1-940119-23-6

ISBN, Kindle Edition: 978-1-940119-24-3

Library of Congress Catalog Number: 2019915398

Ordering & Queries: info@rucksackpress.com

Cover design by Bonnie Donaghy. All other trademarks and copyrights are property of their respective owners.

This is a work of fiction. All of the characters, organizations, events, and references portrayed in this story are either used fictitiously or are products of the author's imagination. Any resemblance to real persons, entities, or organizations is purely coincidental.

Find a mistake? Corrections are welcome and often rewarded. Email the publisher at editor@rucksackpress.com.

anthonystclair.com | rucksackuniverse.com

SPECIAL FEATURES

Go behind the scenes of the Rucksack Universe:

Check out the Special Features
Become a patron for behind-the-scenes special access

Reading Order
The Rucksack Universe is an ongoing, non-sequential series. Read
it in any order you like. If you want to know the order of release
or the order of the storylines, here are suggested reading orders:

Choose your reading itinerary
rucksackuniverse.com/reading-order

ABOUT THE AUTHOR

Anthony St. Clair creates compelling fiction and non-fiction for a curious world full of everyday discoveries, endeavors, and surprises. He is the author of the ongoing Rucksack Universe series; covers craft beer, food, business, and more for various publications; and is a copywriter and content manager for select clients. When not at his desk or in his kitchen in Oregon, Anthony is on an adventure with his wife, son, and daughter.

For more information:

rucksackuniverse.com | anthonystclair.com

instagram.com/rucksackuniverse

twitter.com/anthonystclair

facebook.com/anthony.stclair.author

pinterest.com/anthonystclair

amazon.com/author/anthonystclair

goodreads.com/anthonystclair

youtube.com/anthonystclairauthor

bookbub.com/authors/anthony-st-clair

9 781940 119229